James Ward Kirk
PUBLISHING

Surreal Nightmares

Book © James Ward Kirk Publishing

Edited by Sebastian Crow and James Ward Kirk

Internet: http://www.jwkfiction.com
Twitter: @jameswardkirk
Facebook: James-Ward-Kirk-Fiction

Cover art © John D. Stanton 2016
Cover Design by John D. Stanton
Interior illustrations by Gidion Van de Swaluw © 2016

ISBN-13: 978-0692684962 (James Ward Kirk Publishing)

ISBN-10: 0692684964

Contents

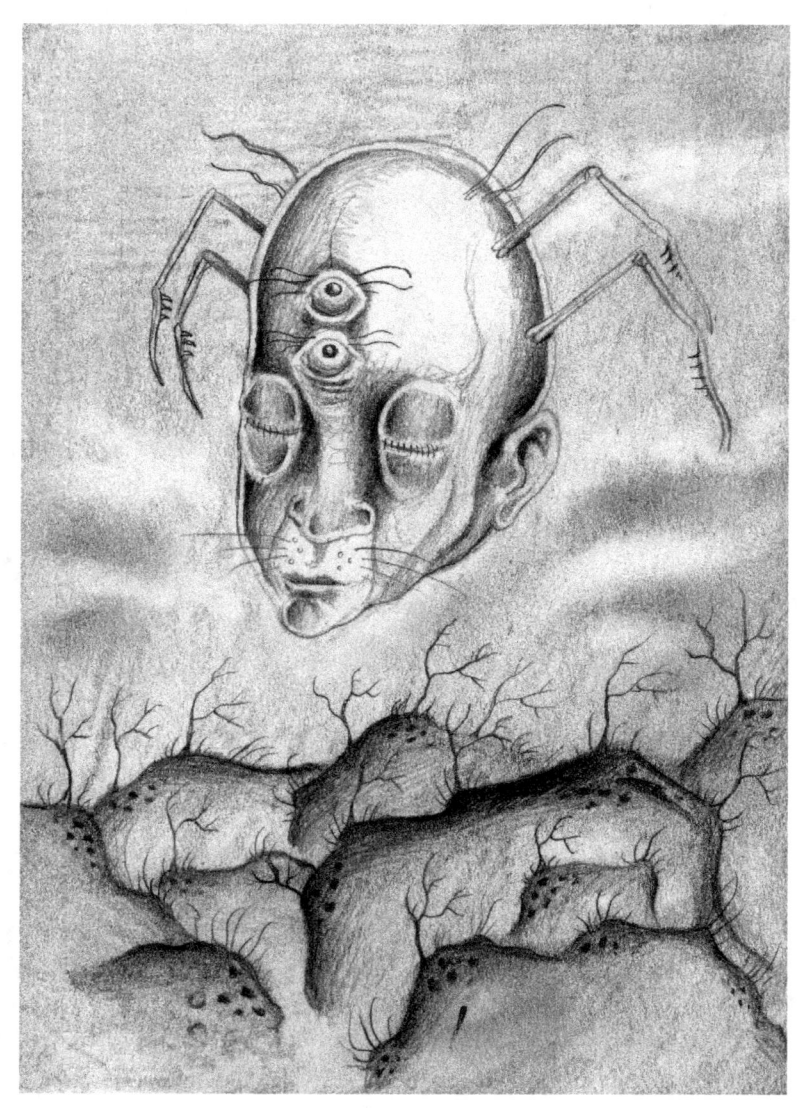

Mathias Jansson

Dream of Phineas P. Gage

Woke up by the pain, by the iron rod penetrating my brain.
I could feel the taste of brain in my mouth
The feeling of blood, gore, and bone dripping down my throat
In my fist, I held the rod still stained with blood and brain

Shattered memories flickering on my retina, the rock, the hole, the powder, the hot sun in my eyes, the sledge, the explosion, the warm wind in my face, a sudden pain in the head and the numb feeling of silence, timeless wandering around talking with people, waiting for the doctor. The fingers poking in my head, eyes gazing down the hole in my scull seeing my teeth and tongue. Blood on the bed, someone passes out by the sight, screams, people running in the stairs, and suddenly the low voices around me, the whispering in the corners. I can see bizarre creatures, abnormal characters sneaking around in the shadows. They look angry, anxious, lost, looking with fear at me, afraid to approach, shying when the see the iron rod in my hand. Suddenly I can feel a cold liquid is running through my brain, water, or antiseptic, flushing down sticky brain matter, gore and some bites of bone from the cracked skull into my mouth and throat. But I cannot feel any more fear and pain. Rather, I realize I am smiling, chatting happily with the doctor and his assistant standing by the bed.

My family and friends they say I am no longer Gage
Perhaps they think I am insane
That the rod blows out my brain
But it's not true, I am not insane or mad
Rather the iron rod cast out all my insanity
Pushed it out in to the real world
My nightmares and fears released
Ghosts, bad memories or nightmares, call it what you will,
released by an accident
Now sneaking in the shadows, following every step I take
My name is Phineas P. Gage
I walk; I sleep and eat with my iron rod in my hand

It's the only thing my nightmare creatures fears
If they could, they would crawl back from where they came
And fill my split brain with insanity
Because they fear the real world
But I on the other hand have no fears

Are you certain you wish to continue?

Dona Fox

Mama's Jewels and Daddy's Eggs

I didn't want to kill my daddy outright so I squinted my eyes in the early morning light to ensure no poison-covered blackberry leaves ended up in my apron. Only the tiny yellow crazy-making flowers were destined for my daddy's belly. I searched for the same flowers I'd seen Nibi eating—right before she went mad.

I don't think nobody else saw her odd gyrations the day she fell dead in the field, wobbly legs trembling, long ears flapping-- chewing on the chickens, tossing the ducks in the air; she went plumb crazy, right before she ate the blackberry bushes by the road. Moyne County had sprayed those blackberries with poison to keep the vines from covering the highway. After she ate the blackberries, it wasn't long before my goat died, quick and terrible. I cried, I stomped my feet. Daddy wouldn't do anything about it. Said he had to stay on the right side of the County, as he had to work with them. I just got another whipping on top of my goat being dead.

I was a child, I let that pass, but that was a long time ago-I'd suffered at Daddy's hands and his words too many more times. My tolerance had broken.

I didn't want a quick death for Daddy. I wanted to see him in a helpless state as I had been. I wanted him behind bars, in a straightjacket--before he died.

My skirt was soaking wet from the dew, sticking to my legs, and to the open welts on my thighs. The searing pain that resulted set my resolve even more. I couldn't wait for dinner. I'd make him a big omelet for breakfast with these tiny yellow petals hidden in the golden yolks. For good measure, I'd swing back through our woods and throw in a few of the toadstools the townies liked to steal.

I circled the remains of my old goat; I owed her for the inspiration. Hanks of hair still clung to her bones. She was a stubborn one, that Nibi. A bone cracked beneath my bare foot, Nibi always had something to say.

Must have been the bacon grease. I spooned the gray-green oil out of the old can we always kept on the back of the stove. The smooth globs melted and sizzled in the big iron skillet--eyeballs without the colored parts. The smell of the grease filled the air, woke my brothers--called them down to breakfast.

Mama made me enlarge the omelet. Big enough to feed her and my three brothers, too. In addition, she made me take a plate. She's always saying I'm too skinny.

Didn't expect the whole family for breakfast. Well, it wasn't everybody. Daddy didn't show. He was out working one of his cases. All night. Again. Dammit.

Mama, tickled to have her boys around her, felt pleased I made breakfast on my own. She was happy Daddy wasn't there. She had me bring out the flowered plates. She went back to her to her room and got dressed a little prettier. I swear she put on every piece of jewelry she owned.

"This is like a party," she said. "Let's eat."

The boys were ready. They were always hungry.

I bit my thumb. These were supposed to be Daddy's eggs.

"Come on, Ginger, serve your omelet."

So, I did.

I slid a portion of the glistening eggs onto each flowered plate. Tiny yellow petals and bits of mushroom taunted me from within the folds of the omelet. I hadn't even circled the table before my brothers hunched over their plates and began to shove the crazy-making food into their mouths.

"Sit down, Ginger, eat." My mama clenched my wrist and pulled me to my chair.

I picked up my fork and laid a small bite on my tongue.

My tongue twisted in my mouth.

The bare cement floor cracked.

My brothers' mouths spun

Black vinyl records

Red needle tongues

Drawing words from the air

Edison, Victor, Victrola

Too slow to ken my kin

Where's the dog to hear

His master's voice . . .

My handsome brothers

Went on record

distorted . . . scratched, Old Scratch

they made a pact with Him

I covered my eyes and screamed

6

Mama Mama Mama . . .
She was staring at her jewelry . . .
Talking to her jewelry . . .

Swaying, chanting, drugged–my mama:

> I hold the dreams, the oeuvres
> of mes oeufs--locked in boxes
> Mama's jewelry – shall I
> Frame them, pin them on the
wall

> Step near, feel my warmth
> My breath on your cheek
> again, Look closely . . .

My oldest brother, bent at Mama's side, entranced by the object she presented:

> This one is a bracelet
> Gleaming on my wrist
> Each jewel is a woman
> There's a dozen women
> Appearing to
> Dance maypole
> In an alley their
> Hearts ripped
> from their chests
> Still beating,
> consumed by my dark son
> dressed and propped
> on wooden stakes

"Yes, Mama." My oldest brother kissed her cheek, wiped drool from his lips, and was gone as if he had received his orders.

> And here, the gems
> In my tiara,

Mama crushed my middle brother to her,

> twenty women

by hay hooks hung
from the brick walls
of a tenement -
flowers gracing the gray alley
chiffon dresses -- oops, one
fell out
now my handsome child is
caged to die.

Tears ran down his face–and Mama's face–as they held each
other. Then he growled, "Damn bitches," spun and left.

My pale white rings
gifted to me
by my favorite son,

She crooked her finger and my youngest, most tender brother
floated to my mama. He kissed her hand then held it against his
heart as she continued,

he chewed his way
through mermaids.
They drown, you know,
in the proper fluid.

I could feel his laughter in the room for hours.

Now my children
Are locked in boxes
Yet to be poisoned
Waiting for fitting
into a proper crown
my bloody jewels
My Oeuvre.

A barred door opens, I pass through, and the bars clang shut
behind me
    I walk down a long, narrow tunnel–it is dark, chill, and close.
    A heavy metal door with but one tiny window opens–
    I pass through the door, it seals shut behind me
    with a whoosh of air–the heavy lock engages,
    I'm in an airless, dim corridor where I am

8

Near sightless and again I shuffle
until I pass through another
heavy door that locks
behind me, then a
warm and humid
corridor and
another and
another
until
I
realize
I can't breathe
And there is no way out.
Alive.

I remember the man. There was a man, Ovidian? Mama said, Ovid, you've changed. I have to remember the man. I'm crawling on unfamiliar damp cement. It smells of urine. I'm beginning to remember the man, his poetry, his threats, what he will do to the others if any of us tell. Perhaps he was Ophidian. For we must all play along.

I'm looking for the one. In a tiny cage, pressed against the wall. Or, the one that paces.

But this cage is full of women dancing Maypole. The pole in the center of the cage is decked in flowers. There is an overabundance of tiny yellow petals. Hundreds of multicolored ribbons drape from the top of the Maypole into the women's hands.

The women wear garlands of yellow flowers in their hair. Their gauzy white dresses and flowing hair bounce as they pass each other ducking up and down in the intricate dance required to weave the ribbons around the pole.

A flower of dark blood has soaked the front of each white dress. Each dancer has an open hole where her heart should be.

Blood dribbles from his mouth and hands; he has just gorged. He wipes his face. He rubs his hand on his pant leg. More blood appears on his lip. The women laugh and continue to weave the Maypole ribbons around him. Tighter. Tighter.

His face is turning red.

He grabs for the ribbons.

He strains to pull them from his neck.

The women lace the strands across his face.

A shadow falls over the cage.
I slip under the bars.

The next cage is filled with a yellowish fluid.

Mermaids float on their backs in the liquid, arms hanging lax beneath them. Pale eyes appear sightless for no iris shows, white scales float from their bodies into the fluid, and their fins are simply gone. Their fingers spread beneath them -- lifeless or reaching, searching for the man, oh please, let the mermaids be alive, let their fingers be splayed in a vengeful search for the man who sits huddled in the corner laughing. Surrounded by white plastic bottles--laughing.

I slip into the cage to accost him.

Coughing, choking, tears streaming from my eyes, I leave, for-- like mermaids--I cannot breathe bleach.

The third cage is taller inside than out.

I've heard that's possible.

Three, four stories high. Gray bricks line the walls.

Women in chiffon dresses are somehow affixed and hanging from the bricks at various heights. Each dress is a different pastel color; there are no gem tones here. Blooming flowers hung upside down as high as I can imagine.

As I stare, one falls. I'm sure she is dead, yet with a push and a tilt, I pull the hook from her back. It's a hay hook--we used them on the farm. Horrible, dangerous tools.

My most handsome brother could juggle five of them at a time. He always said he was going to run away and join the circus--as the saying goes. I wonder if there are really circuses looking for handsome hay hook juggling farm boys. I wonder if he took to killing women and hanging them on alley walls in chiffon dresses instead.

As I was examining the hook, she must have crawled away . . . I had no chance to find her. If my brother did this, she could turn him in . . . He was so handsome, you would just have to say the name of the famous actor he resembled, and every woman would remember seeing him. His good looks were probably how he caught so many women, put them in chiffon dresses, and hung them on the alley wall.

As I said, I had no chance to find her. The one that got away.

Laying on the cold cement floor.

Dead. Skull crushed.
My eyes open, unseeing. I had been so young, so innocent.
I reached down and touched my face--cold.
I should have had a life. I was cheated. I cried for me.
A chuckle.
Head swivel.
My murderer.
Inclined on his bunk,
Cheshirery grin on his face.
I showed him the hay hook
he got the point,
Took it to heart, he did.
My attorney says, I don't know what I knew or when I knew it
vis-a-vis the hook still being in my hand.
[*I say, I don't know if I even realized I still had the hook in my*
hand.]
That will be argued.

My father came once--out of uniform.
In the dark night.
Saw all of us in one visit.

We're our mama's children.
He won't be associated with us.
He tried to discipline us; she wouldn't have it.
He's never done wrong by us.
And . . .
He won't come again.

--all stiff and formal, as if there
wasn't a hay hook in his chest.

Don't ask me if I'm sorry.

Mama, didn't do anything wrong either,
My eggs freed her and changed her–
she's ran off with a poet.
I think I mentioned him earlier.
[*Though I wasn't supposed to.*]

It was all about the environment.
Well, it was, wasn't it?

11

It was about the environment,
and politics, if you will.

Aaron Vlek

Some Thoughts on the Blind Owl

I
The Object

The slender volume lay at rest in my lap. It seemed purposely deceptive. It could have been asleep, or dead. It might have been poised to leap from the safety of my body onto the exposed throat of some nearby prey. Other people would never give it a second glance if they saw it hiding in the dust upon my shelf. Seeing its delicate silhouette among so many others of its seeming kind, most might have even thought it trivial.

Now, I don't regret its coming into my possession. Many others have come to possess—no, have come to be possessed *by*—this small gift from a stranger.

I feel its pulse, a foreign cadence filling my chest with a hollow glow, beating the strange rhythm of its unhuman heart. It calls to me from the unfathomed pit of my own deepest, un-manifested self, a monotonous fevered drone igniting my blood. The insect buzzing of a million machines sings a chorus of mindless, frenzied motion. It's as familiar to me as my own voice, whispering secrets into my ear from the darkest stairwell of my soul's misgivings. It's a greedy, jealous discovery that I must share. But with whom?

The truth is the monstrous heart of this tiny object of paper and ink—cradled in my lap like a forever-dying child—has killed. It has compelled many beings, tender flesh and blood, to expel their own life from their young bodies with a single self-willed act of violence. At first when I heard this, I sneered inwardly and laughed aloud. I see now. This twilight essence is a sacred artifact, like a protected savage child; willing to kill, able to set free, not caring to which shore its poisoned lips intoxicates.

Hedayat, the blind god who birthed this holy monster killed himself after giving it birth, after letting it fly upon the world. Like the praying mantis, it kills its mate and consumes him. This creator god mated deep within the unsanctified self and procreated a sacrament of madness, a method and a map, a maze, a formula and a means to no knowable end. This is an unapproachable horizon in a forever twilight landscape where the only movement is that of shadows.

The small object slumbers darkly but emits a noxious fume. Blind to the world, I am consumed. I have been here before, but I am not seduced, I am reminded, of home. I reach out and caress its spine with the languor of sweet despair for its poisoned ink already floods my veins. It mocks me like a torturer whom I invite into my own bed. My womb bleeds such young as this, which its creator gave his life to bear.

The pages flutter silently like the wings of the cicadas of evil on nights when it is too thick to sleep. The object awakens fully to my desire for it, and it yields. I have sated myself on its blood many times, yet I hunger still for more. This hunger can never be fulfilled, never know satiety. Only the death of the mind can still this craving. Only the knowledge of this craving brings joy.

The small object quickens in my hand as I open it tenderly, like a heart, like a flower, like a book, and I read ...

II
The Observation

I meet Hedayat out walking on a moonlit path to the sometimes home. I stood hard by, silently watching as he drew near then passed me by. My thoughts bore deep upon him, but he did not glance my way. I turned and followed, unnoticed as any shadow.

My hand reached out and lightly touched the sleeve of his coat. It was damp and heavy, and my fingers came away shiny wet. My hands fell to my sides and I couldn't look at them, knowing well the shade those stains would reveal to the morning light.

"Read what I have written!" I called out, but my voice was swallowed by cold silence.

"You were in the grave eighty-nine sunsets on the day I was born," I called out after him.

He smiled a strange little smile that crushed my mind and froze deep into my soul like the dull edge of a rusted knife.

"I was born in a grave," he whispered. "And you know nothing."

"I live in a graveyard," I countered. "Where dancing corpses walk by day, but in the night gangrene devours the brittle bloodless souls. They walk so the blind larvae can feed without regret."

He stopped walking and looked at me for the first time. I tried to hand him my papers, my precious stories, poems, my ancient legends told anew, but he cast them sharply aside where they fluttered slowly to the ground like the dried wings of albino moths.

He locked my eyes with his own and slowly, delicately, peeled away my coat, as a physician would remove the blood soaked robe from a cadaver. His fingers were so long and thin, and white as bone. Underneath his touch, I was all Nothingness.

"You have grown fat and drunk," he replied. "On ancient nectar stolen from the tombs of my ancestors, but the blood of your own pen glistens in the moonlight like the trail of snails along the dark leaves of the opium poppy," he said softly, as though it pleased him. Then he emitted a cold unhuman laugh that reminded me of nothing but the scream of the jackal when it scents its prey.

He turned from me, his boots crushing the virginal husks of my discarded words into the frozen mud of eternal decay. I gathered up myself and followed, knowing each step that he would take, but one. I have been here before.

"I saw the picture," I said, my voice a hollow echo, my breath a dripping icy vapor on the still night air.

He paused, his eyes forward into the embrace of a darkness ready to swallow him forever from my sight. He could not have heard me.

"You looked drunk they said, or asleep. But the body looked to me like one sated, unconscious from too much lust in its blood. Tell me, when you knew that you were finally dead by your own hand, into whose arms did you surrender in that dark mist? What came for you that last night, and left the body behind looking that way?"

II

The Conversation

"So, what do you want from me?" he asked.

"I'm not completely sure yet," I replied.

"There's nothing to see, it's all there in the book you read."

"No, that was just a stream. I would drink from the cistern subterranean," I insist.

"But I am dead."

"No, we're talking right now, you and me."

"No, I am dead; this conversation is taking place in your head."

"Have you never picked up an old photograph, scratched and worn, a corner missing, another torn, only to recognize pieces of a secret place only few may find as addicts to a fog drenched alley?"

"Are you trying to evoke my interest?" he asks. "I was beyond that long ago."

"No, I'm a jackal," I say, One who recognizes things and consumes them—fuels one and all, nothing more."

"Okay, then, what about the jackals?"

"Your black dogs, watchers, guardians of the threshold," I say quickly. "They were jackals of course. So were your drunken policemen."

"How many were there? Watchers of what threshold? And what do they watch?" he demands, growing impatient with my impertinence.

"The secret Rubicon, The Styx, the way through to the other side. Called Da'ath by the Jews. They watch to keep those from entering who have not been called," I say quickly before he has time to cut me off my words. "They are the veil!"

"And what river is this?"

"Your poisoned wine! Having already murdered all that was human in yourself, all that was left was the pure formalities of flesh!"

"Perhaps you're reading an awful lot into my little story," he says smiling, but his eyes are cold, disinterested in all I say.

"Every piece of imagery you employed just happened to fit snug as the only key in the only lock in the only town?"

"What do you want from me?" he demands. "Besides trying to make me think you are clever, which I do not."

"I would salute you, for achieving a place in writing where pen and ink disappear like a window where there is no glass. There are others of course, and I collect them. I know when my own pen runs out of glass, and fills instead with wine, or poison.

"So we'll raise our empty glass and toast this great genius. How lucky we are," he sneers. "Now I'll take my leave."

"No, wait!"

"Why?"

"Why? Why am I feeling like a confessor before a defrocked priest?" I ask, trying anything I can think of to keep him from fading from my sight.

"A strange question," he replies.

"This conversation is infuriating."

"Then I'll go," he says, turning his back to me.

"Not yet, I won't allow it," I say, my voice lowered to a growl.

"And you'll stop me—how?"

"Because this conversation is all in my head."

"I see! Then tell me of the canker that eats the soul like a crystallized colony of square roots, neutralizing the acids and salts of the sacred architecture of your own sacrificial city of the dead," he says, looking at me for the first time and I allow myself to believe . . . seeing me.

"It's an evil that I cannot overcome," I admit, sadly, "A stigma, a stain, a shroud that binds my pen. An ogre, a tyrant, a blindness of my own," I whisper.

"And its name is?" he asks softly.

"Innocence."

"Innocence is never a tyrant," he says, his voice swelling with anger.

"I mean rather an innocence like the virgin's hand."

"Meaning?"

"Meaning the bridge between the lands dark and light, and in-between, sacrificing, what is no sacrifice, I pursued this light and dark relentlessly, now the supplicant in silence, now the rapist with blood stained hands, now the seducer of abominations, now the subservient whore, always the self-cloistered one in pursuit of the only lover there can ever be," I finish my litany and look to him.

"And yet ...,"

"And yet?"

"Tell me about the river, the stream, as it appears and disappears."

"It's another loss of virginity, where humans become a distraction as you touch the brutal intimacy of the Self. One can never return to the safety of the dying campfire of our ancestors. We peer into the blackness beyond that protecting human light. The bestial eyes that stare back at us from the hidden places are our own, luring us out to the solitary hunt."

I ask, "And what of language?"

"Yes what of the habituated patterns of communication that strangle us?" he replies without glancing at me. "What of the monkey chatter that passes for human communication but really only assures the frightened primate he is not alone. What of the monotonous drone of our own worthless thoughts? These syncopations of suffocation?" he demands, turning to look my way, his eyes drunk with accusation.

"But what of the poisoned wine that intoxicates and kills?" I say, parrying his thrust and hoping to sound clever.

"It kills the monkey," he replies, as if it should be obvious, "Stilling the metronome of his chatter. It kills the monkey and frees the Other, the Shadow.

Only by breaking down, disrupting, always adding something unexpected can the mind descend out of the world."

"Read what I have written," I cry out like an impatient child begging for candy, dying for his glance upon the hot folds on my soul.

"Perhaps later. What about the knife?" he says casually.

"Yes!" I say. "I kept thinking of the *pesh khent* knife, the birthing dagger, the blade the Jackal uses to open the mouths of the dead."

"And the geometric shapes?"

"The city of black pyramids," I reply, satisfied with myself.

"Egypt?" His voice is cold like one who is tired of playing.

"No, long before that, not before, outside. Those who passed The River for the last time, willingly and by their own hand, built for themselves a black pyramid, in the city of Pyramids," I say, my voice breathless, paced and careful as though reciting from a long dead memory. "But I have never been there. Who build your black pyramid?"

"I do not know, how can one know such things? But when you say willingly *by their own hand*, you mean—"

"No, I mean they unhooked the girders of the self, let the pieces fall until there was nothing left but stars and blackness, and then nothing left at all."

"What of the spectral horses?" he asks, his black eyes narrowing as though he sees me for the first time.

"There is a Horse, a spectral Horse, whose shadow falls across a thing and it withers and dies, a horse no human rider may mount, a horse at whose center there dances a sentient black flame."

"And you think I wrote of this Horse?" he says with a laugh incredulous.

"I think you did!"

"What of the strange laughter then, the coughing, the hollow unhuman sounds that pour from dark throats that hold no living breath?"

"Connectors, warning lights, door bells, calling cards and the Tunnels! Of Set," I say, triumphant. I must surely have him now. "Signals and wormholes—the corners that must be turned. Hear the laugher, the coughing, and the River cannot be far. The laughter and the knife are connected," I declare as I close my litany and draw a breath to steady myself.

"The black dogs?" he says, a drill sergeant of the obscene where only nakedness is our uniform and rank.

"And the policemen," I reply. "All connected, and the woman and the blood, the poison wine and the perpetual twilight, the old man and the child, the girl and the crone, all connected."

"How?" he asks simply, his voice now sad and pale.

"All of these elements produce the Babe in the Abyss," I answer, wondering why the tears lick the corners of my eyes.

"And what exactly is that?" he prompts, as though we have been through this ritual a thousand times before.

"You."

"I?"

"The Babe in the Abyss is a Hermetic formula. Look most carefully at its description. Always it is a child, assuming the sign of silence; the sign performed by placing the tip of the index finger against the front teeth, and smiling.

It signifies that one cannot speak of what they have seen across the River. But those that have been there will always recognize you."

"And you think I knew of this imagery?" His voice almost makes me falter in my resolve. But I hold fast.

"I think people who travel frequently to Antarctica will always speak of whiteness and cold, and black water that kills. And I think that clever men who study in Paris in the early 20th century are likely to come across all manner of strange creatures and their writings," I say, my voice now coy and playful as I know of what I speak and bluff my way through the minefield of his thoughts. "But the Babe in the classical renderings . . ." I steel myself, and continue. "Always has its right hand against its teeth but yours has the left hand. I think we have two hands for a reason."

"And what of the Bitch?"

"The anima of the secret self, the shadow," I cry out, delighted to have regained my composure. "In the Twilight world, the Bitch represents the road to dissolution, the Stations of the Black

Cross, the landmarks of the interior landscape in which appetite, weakness, passion, sin, and crime, are embraced, consumed, and expended as exhaust. The corpse is the body of the dead human self, the husk. When you die before you die, you must always carry this with you," I declare and hope this it is true,

"And the exhaust?"

"The painting, the poetry, the prose, the sacraments of the soul that those who never cross the River must always seek out and long for but never produce from within themselves."

"What else about the Bitch?" he asks.

"She is The World, the whore who gives herself to every common fool, yet she is forever beyond the grasp of those who would leave her behind."

"One cannot take strange lovers to their bed and then play with the toys of a child. What else?" he asks.

"The Bitch is the Soul, tempting, seducing, elusive. It pollutes the sanity with cankers. Sanity is the first lie to be abandoned, nothing more than the virgin's robe at sunset on the night of her wedding. She will remove it willingly and with joyful abandon, or have it dragged from her soft flesh by an impatient hand. The Bitch is the Soul, at once the most beautiful secret self, and the most repulsive dried up lecher. A sensual secret with an icy hand, monstrous, toothless, a breath that both repels and intoxicates."

"And the fever?

"Threshold sickness," I say. "Or insanity, however one must to see it."

"And what of the meat?"

"That which is not done away with quickly will putrefy. Cross the river willingly, but try to maintain a place in the world, and gangrene will set in, the sores that eat away the mind like a canker. Tell me Hedayat, did you go willingly into the darkness that last time? Or did madness and intoxicants carry you unconscious over the threshold like a drunken bride?"

"What you ask is not yours to hear. What of the Cobra, and the indistinguishable twins?"

"Ouroboros."

"And the twins, one light, one dark, yet the same?" he asks, testing me now and demanding that I answer from my place of darkness.

"The Mother was the Cobra, and the venom her milk. The Bitch would never allow herself to be kissed, but she herself gave the one and only kiss necessary."

"So you have it all figured out?" he says, the tongue of contempt flicking again at his words.

"Yes, I have it all figured out, but everyone who reads *The Blind Owl* gets to figure it out too. But it will never be the same. It's the oddly wrapped present that one finds hidden on a top shelf in the back of their closet. Tear open the wrapping, and find a mirror inside, and marvel at the strange beauty, or the unfathomable horror, and the impossible likeness to yourself."

"It seems you have found what you sought," he says, turning from him as if to continue alone.

"I believe you are right."

"Good, then I must end this conversation and be on my way."

"Indeed, and I am finished, so I will bid you a good twilight Sir."

"And to you as well madam, see you on Doomsday!" he says, waving with his back already turned to me and then he is gone, swallowed once again by the black mists that rise from a sea of graves that look to innocence as rows of black marble pyramids.

William Cook

September Ripe Tomatoes

Gazing skyward, I trace the gradient of the shape's descent. It falls slowly, almost languidly. As it flicks past each of the tower block's smoking levels, it grows in size. From a dark smudge, it assumes shape in its steep approach. The shape twists slowly in the buffeting updraft. The sombre cloth billows upwards from its weight, flapping like a flag in a hurricane, as it falls. All around, noise swells and builds, like the relentless onslaught of the tide underneath a sodden jetty. Sirens, screams, and strange plopping noises, like stones dropped into a deep well, pierce the monotonic wall of sound. I watch her fall, because it is apparent that the shape is female, her limbs are flailing as she descends more rapidly now. As she rolls in the air to her side, her long hair is electrified, stood on end at a right angle as is her long dress. As she reaches the third level with speed, I glimpse her swollen belly. A nanosecond of life. By the time my mind barks - *'Oh my God!'* . . . she hits the street. Twenty meters away from me, I hear the *whump/splat*. The same queer plopping sound that all the other falling bodies have been making as they hit the hard surface. As she hits, she seems to flatten – to merge with the grey, dust-caked street – her pregnant form atomically collapsed for an instant. And as she bounces, like a wet dishcloth on linoleum, something florid erupts from her gut like a worm bursting forth from a ripe apple. It spins across the asphalt and jerks to a halt as the umbilical cord stretches to full capacity like a bungee cord, snapping the glistening pink ball of flesh backwards. I am numb, but I manage to make a step forward. The surrounding noise is a dull hellish roar and my lungs labour for clean air, the dust swirls around me like a fog. Filled with dread, I approach the bloody shape, curled in on itself, and gently roll it over with my shoe. I stagger back – its eyes burn an incandescent blue up at me from where it lay hunched. The face is twisted in an indescribable grimace and its sharp teeth gnash together – the slick pink skin, more of a red hue up close, peels back from its teeth as its forked tongue lashes and twirls like a snake's tail from its open mouth. Two horns, extended above its eye sockets on its large blood-caked forehead, seem to have grown an inch since I first laid eyes upon the hideous creature. As it starts to consume the umbilical cord still attached to its belly, I turn to flee and promptly stumble over another exploded corpse. I pick myself up, barely able to breath now – the sounds of more dull thuds and plopping noises resound all around like muffled artillery explosions – as I watch the creature eat its way towards its mother, lustily devouring the slick life-line as it drags itself closer. I turn – slowly, almost imperceptibly, as if afraid of what might happen next – and run like hell, deep into the swirling clouds of smoke and ash, leaping over split, burst, bodies scattered like so many squashed ripe tomatoes, as the remaining light fades to black.

A. Henry Keene

Filthy Water Flows

Moonlit fog swirls like grey paisley patterns around my ankles as I slosh and slog through the rain-soaked muck and weeds. *Fwoop. Fwoop.* Each slurping step churns my stomach. It feels as though it is filled with mating snakes, and I'm on the verge of vomiting. Perhaps it is not so much the sound as the situation that has me nauseous. My father is missing, and I've got to find him. I bow my head and strain my eyes to see the sloppy clay trail. No footprints, but I have a clue he came this way. His truck sits a hundred yards back in the spot where he used to park when he brought me here. That was thirty-five or forty years ago. He doesn't know that. For him it might be like forty minutes. He's lost in time. He may know where he is, but he doesn't know when. He may even be searching for me down at our old fishing spot. That's where I'm headed. I scan the field toward the river to see trees and the tips of weeds above the ground-hugging fog. A light breeze bends the rain-soaked weeds, and I recall him bringing me here to fly kites when I was a boy.

I hold the spool of string in my small hands, which move about in response to the bright red kite in the dark grey sky. I watch it soar with its long white tail, whipping along behind. When my father kneels behind me, his stubble brushes my tender cheek and my ear to make a loud scruffy sound, and chills travel through my body like electricity through copper wire.

He says, "You gotta feel the wind." His voice is deep and gravelly. "When the kite pulls, let some string out." I feel the string dance in my small hands and fight with my skinny arms to keep it from flying away. The kite circles and spins, then I loosen my grip, and string rushes between my thumb and finger. The kite soars up, and I gasp. I want to hold it tight. What if the kite flies into space? I grip the string, but it burns my fingers, and I let it go. My father laughs, as the kite soars ever higher. I try to stop it again, but it is no use. The string simply rips through my weak grip and burns my tender skin. My father laughs, and fear shakes me as though I've been brought before a fairytale king to answer for my misdeeds. My skin kinda ripples along my body, and I feel ashamed.

I return my gaze to the darkening grey sky. There is no kite. Only clouds and the brightening moon. I ask myself where I'm going then answer that I'm headed to the river. Why am I going there? Gotta find my father. He may be there looking for his little boy. He may be calling my name as though I'm lost.

Starting down a slight hill, I remind myself to be careful on this slippery trail, and the next step in the rain-soaked slop slides out from under me. I fall onto my back. Air escapes through my lips in a startled hiss. It seems to travel forever into the endless dusk and damp of this weedy place. I lay in the mess and struggle to catch my breath. After a few minutes, I turn to get up on an elbow and feel something firm and flat in the slop under my hand. I pick it up. A worn black leather wallet: misshaped and overstuffed. I flip it open to reveal my father, looking back at me.

His eyes beam with simple joy behind oversized, black-rimmed glasses. My heart thumps, and heat rushes through my body. I'm on the right path. He's been here. Fell at the same spot and lost his wallet. He could be injured. Gotta move. Gotta find him before he dies in this November rain.

I move carefully down the path toward the river until it steepens, then slow my pace even more. Desperate to maintain my footing, I reach out, grasping the weeds for balance and turn sideways to avoid another fall. Could he have managed this descent? Where else could he have gone? The thicket is undisturbed to either side, and the trail hasn't split. When the path levels out, I pick up the pace and push on into even colder air and thicker fog toward the river. I'm headed to our old fishing spot. I'll know it by the gnarled tree with a massive trunk that splits into three.

Rustling in the weeds nearby. I freeze. My heart freezes. Time freezes.

"Dad?"

A low groan rumbles through the weeds.

My moon-cast shadow plays on the weeds before me, as I draw a long, deliberate breath and peer into the thicket. The tangled web of low brush, thistles, and pope berries looks like a Jackson Pollock painting. It draws me ever deeper into its intertwining, matted mess, and I feel myself sinking deeper into it until my eyes flutter, and I hear my father's voice, low and growling,

"You could fuck up a one-car pauper funeral."

I hear the jingling of his belt buckle. It rings out like the tolling of some ancient bell of atonement, and I feel the time has come for me to burn. I would be the sacrifice to make everything right in the world, and I should be honored, but all I feel is the terrible trembling of my hands and the breath caught in my throat. My clinched fists shake, and I bite my lip until blood flows down my chin.

"For your own good." His drunken slur is thick with bourbon.

He reaches back and the belt arcs below his clinched fist. Then he swings, and I hear the slap of leather and feel the belt bite into the flesh of my leg. It snaps like a bullwhip made of lightening. It burns like an acid attack and Medusa's gaze. It is the very definition of pain inflicted by my cherished caretaker. My body jerks, as my muscles spasm. I try to run, but he has me by the arm. He hauls me around for another shot. I feel the strap again, and molten lava boils through me. I become a pulsating reactor filled with plutonium and ammonia and bleach and baking soda and vinegar and, my God, I'm about to explode with love and fear and anger and confusion, and deep down I feel the hatred. It is dense like a black hole and heavy like a dead man's eyelids.

As the vision fades, a tremulous breath lingers long in my throat. Again, I hear rustling in the weeds. Nervous energy drips from my fingertips, and I extend a trembling hand into the thicket, push the weeds to one side, and step off the trail.

I walk slowly toward the rustling sound, as my chest and throat tingle. Weeds bend beneath my feet, as each step brings me closer to the source of the sound. Was it him? Fallen, ill, decrepit and near death? Was it a ruined cat, car-struck and gut-busted? I step again into the vast expanse of weedy wilderness, and something bolts. Something large and dark scrambles away. My body jerks and freezes and my heart thumps heavily in my chest. Steam billows from my open mouth, and a siren wails. Where did it go? What was it? It looked hu--

I stand for a long moment and breathe slowly. When my heart settles I renew my dedication to the task. I've gotta find him. Gotta keep moving toward the river. I'll find him at the old spot. The spot where-- Something dark and heavy crept into my soul and curled around like a cat about to nap. Tears trickle down my cheeks. I swallow hard, walk deliberately back to the path, and rub a hand across my face. Gotta get my shit together.

At the path, I turn right and walk the slick clay through the high weeds until I reach the highest riverbank. After a final steep and tree-lined descent, I look over the edge into the dense fog where I know the river flows. I can't see it but hear it slosh its dross and filth downstream. I wonder if it ever stops? The unrelenting flow of dead fish, dogs, coal dust, and bits of plastic, which mix and grind up on the shore? I step cautiously toward the precipice, and my foot slides on a slippery mess. Looking down through the fog, I see something around my ankle. My eyes focus to reveal twisted guts, fur, and teeth. Chills rush through my body, and my heart pounds double time. Trying to step back, I fall over the edge. I see the bright moon and feel a heavy thump on my back. My neck and back bend, a heavy blow blasts my mouth, and I roll to the bottom.

Disoriented, breathing heavily, I search the fog for the moon but find no bright spot. My head aches, and warm blood flows down my cheek. I try to raise a hand to touch it but can't. My whole body is tightly bound by something moist and rubbery. I am wrapped up in guts, and no matter how I struggle against the sinews I remain bound. My limbs shake with the effort until they collapse, and I lose consciousness for a bit. When I come to, I hear a low snarl. It is the sound of a clogged drain giving way. The gurgling rush of water through filthy pipes. My eyes spring open, and I struggle against the guts. Sweat stings my eyes and my stomach convulses, as the gurgling sound grows louder. Desperate to free myself, I bend my head to the side and bite into the stringy intestines across my right shoulder. I tear, gnash, and rip and growl until my teeth shred the last strands, and my right arm works free. Meanwhile the gurgling thing shows itself as a dark figure nearly human in shape. It has arms and legs like a man but stoops over and bends like a stunted tree, whose limbs scrape the ground.

The shadowy form skulks and shambles closer. All around it, the fog glows a thousand colors, which swirl within my soul and drain my strength until I give up the effort to free myself, and the thing reveals itself in a series of images.

Baseballs, belts, and bottles of booze.
The river and wounds that ooze.
My father's smile and angry eyes.
He stands hip deep. The river cries.
Arms straight down. Both hands in water.
Reaching up, the hands of mother.
Red nails scratch and dig in deep.
Into the water, his blood seeps.
He turns his head and looks at me.
Tears flow down his red cheeks.

Sunlight comes. I kick free of the entangling vines, struggle to my feet, and pick up a hefty stick.

Muddy, bloody, and bent, I Stumble along until I see the gnarly tree.

The old man stands, gazing.

"Alex!" His voice decrepit. "Where are ya, son?"

"Over here."

"Been lookin' for ya." He smiles.

"I know." I grip the stick.

"Where ya been?"

"Lost." My chin quivers. My lips compress into a thin line.

"Where's your mother?"

My body shudders, and my neck tenses. I hear sirens and rattlesnakes and car crashes.

I raise the stick and look at his smiling face.

My body tenses, and my arms swing down. Wood shatters, flesh rips, and the old man collapses. His limp jaw hangs to the side. His crooked eyelids droop. I see his blood flow down his cheek onto the dense sand at the river's edge, and without hesitation, I roll him into the filthy water, which barely ripples, as it takes him in and covers him over.

Stephen McQuiggan

Arty Farty

At first, it was kind of funny, waking up so full of wind that the bedsheets flapped like gale tossed sails. He laughed at the sheer exuberance of his flatulence; he sounded like a revving Harley as he dressed, every movement squeezing a growling response from his backside. He was a walking thunderstorm, but as the morning wore on the joke grew thin as the storm showed no sign of abating.

He swallowed a few pills from the medicine cabinet and ate a Spartan breakfast, but the potent gusts still raged forth filling the house with a toxic fug that hung like a heat shimmer on the edge of visibility. Arty began to panic, and when he panicked his guts began to curdle, and when his guts began to curdle...

The smell, a sickly sweet attar, was overpowering. He moved from room to room but the noxious fumes followed like a loyal hound; although ice cracked and flowered on the windowpanes, the house had grown unbearably hot.

Arty expelled another dense wad of burning gas with the sound of a forlorn groan, as if even his sphincter had lapsed into despair; he was producing twisters by lunchtime. He Googled 'Flatulence', but all he came up with were short jokes and long diagnoses. He pondered going to the doctor's but feared he'd clear the waiting room like a one-man drone strike. He would simply have to wait it out – no one ever died from excessive trouser trumpets, did they? Besides, it had started to rain.

He tried to laugh it off. Better out than in, that had always been his father's motto: yes, and when he died Mother said he'd been full of sin and that was what killed him – secretive sin, all bottled up, turning his brain to rotting mush. Sin was better out than in too, that's what she always drilled into him – Let the sin out for all the world to see so that you may be judged.

He emitted a pitiful whine that ruffled his boxers at the thought of the joyless woman who had raised him with slaps and Psalms.

He would have to ride out the storm; it was bound to clear up in a few hours, teatime at the latest. He rang in sick to work – the mere idea of sitting at his desk, puffing out methane and stinking up the office, gave him chills. Jesus, Janey sat at the desk opposite – imagine her reaction if he guffed that sewage on her – how could he ever ask her out after something like that?

His backside parped loudly as if to sonically underline his predicament, the pungent vapours recalling to him his childhood nickname, the one he had hated so much: Arty Farty. Even as a child he had been aware, the name had stuck not because he smelt but simply because it rhymed.

He had run home to Mum once, tripping on his tears, telling her of the taunts that had pursued him there, expecting sympathy. 'You *do* reek!' she'd spat at him. 'You reek of sin just like your Father! The Devil's in you, boy; take care he doesn't set up home there for good.'

It was an inescapable fact – his childhood stank.

'You are what you eat,' had been another of her favourite pearls, and Arty had been gorging on crap; the bin was overflowing with Styrofoam takeaway trays congealed in gravy. It *must* have been something I ate, he reasoned, and following the next logical step decided to evacuate his bowels: if he could rid himself of what had crawled into his colon to die, then surely half the battle was won.

He hurried to the toilet and squatted on it, the porcelain serving as an amplifier, filling the tiny room with the sound of thunder. Sweat broke on him, but no matter how he strained the only thing he passed was more wind. He felt his heart lurch as he pushed with all his might. This is how Elvis died, he thought, they'll find me purple faced with my trousers round my ankles, mummified in my own toxic farts.

He squeezed once more, the sound echoing back off the u-bend like a deflating balloon. He was about to call it quits, to pull up his pants and admit defeat, when, with the growl of a large and vicious dog, his backside unleashed a volley that almost cracked (*Release Me!*) the bowl; one that sounded (*Release Me!*) suspiciously like words.

He gazed down into the small pool of water below as if he might find the answer floating there. Now I'm going crazy into the bargain, he mused; many people have said I talk out of my ass but this is –

The doorbell rang, breaking his reverie. He hurried out, had his hand on the handle, before he realised the extent of his dilemma. His backside let loose a few desultory puffs as if frustrated by his hesitancy. How could he open the front door to anyone and let them smell his eggy pumps?

He peeked through the spyhole and saw his neighbour Lynda on the other side, her face shockingly white beneath the deluge of rain. He was about to ask himself what the hell *she* wanted (she had barely spoken two words to him since she'd moved in six months ago) when he saw she was cradling her toddler, Kevin, the blood still oozing from a gash in his forehead that not even the pelting rain could dilute.

His bowels groaned with the sound of ripping fabric as he turned the key and opened the door; Lynda was already babbling, her incoherent pleas entering the house before she did.

'He was playing Spaceman on the stairs, I've warned him a million times,' she was saying; normally her voice was as robotic as a Speak N Spell, but now she was whiny and animated. 'We need to get him to the hospital, you need to drive us, there's no time to –'

She stopped as the full force of the odour penetrated her frayed senses. She hugged Kevin tighter, turning his face into her chest.

'It's the drains, they must have backed up again with all the rain,' said Arty. 'Wouldn't you be safer phoning for an ambulance?' he asked, desperate to get her back on point.

'There's no time, you'll have to take us.' With that, she was marching down the path into the eye of the gale, waiting by his car as Arty shook a few stray parps from his trouser legs and joined her in the rain. Only when they were both secreted inside his hatchback did Arty appreciate he was trapped in a small box that would soon fill with fetid gastric air.

He thought about lighting a cigarette to mask the fug but worried that the spark of his lighter would ignite and blow the three of them to Kingdom Come. He wound down his window as he gunned the engine but the assault of the weather forced him to put it up again even before Lynda could begin to protest.

This is a nightmare, he thought as he jiggled uncomfortably on his seat; it felt like he was sitting on a molten rivet. He flicked the radio on, playing it loud to drown out the squeaks and squawks of his belaboured sphincter, but Lynda switched off: 'what *is* that smell? Oh my God, it's *disgusting*! What's wrong with you?'

'I must've ate something that disagreed with me,' Arty pouted, trying to keep his eyes on the road as the wipers struggled to clear the sheets of rain. 'I think you should concentrate on what matters here,' he indicated the blanched, bleeding boy on her lap, 'rather than a few bloody farts.'

As if hers smelt of roses, he fumed. He felt his guts churn as he approached a set of traffic lights. As he pulled to a stop, a pistol shot scorched his buttocks and rebounded (*Release Me!*) around the cramped confines of the car.

'What the –' began Lynda, before gagging on the miasma; a thin line of gruel fell down in a rope onto her unconscious son's forehead. Arty was about to apologise when a blast like an industrial hand-dryer tore the seat from his pants (*Release Me!*) and the air inside the car was replaced by a sickly yellow smog.

Lynda slumped forward, her face raw and swollen, as if the touch of that fog had been akin to a fist. He gave her a shake but she just slid off the dashboard onto the gearstick. His first thought was to get out of the car and leave her – to run into the rain, powered by the jet propulsion of wind between his legs – and flee the scene; but then he saw the luminous face of the boy, slack and deathlike, and knew he had to get them to the hospital come hell or high odour.

He wound his window down and drove into the heart of the storm, his stomach cramping with every mile; he felt he was birthing now, crowning some obscenity. When I get to the hospital they'll quarantine me, he fretted, his thoughts flitting from misery to despair in time with the wipers; I'll hit the wards like the goddamn Ebola virus.

Maybe it was a blessing in disguise; maybe when he got Lynda and her boy sorted he could grab a quiet word with a consultant and get himself sorted too. He broke wind, fiery and long, as he pulled into the hospital carpark, but his gas was silent now and that, too, was a blessing; it was Vindaloo hot and painful but its bluster was gone.

Silent But Deadly – that's what they'd called them as kids – SBD's; apt, he thought, for the stench had gained an eye-watering strength, and through the rain and the fug the hospital was little more than a surrealist smudge of blurry light.

'You're full of sin,' he heard his Mother scold, 'and sin is better out than in.' As he navigated his way to the Accident and Emergency entrance he let loose a whisper (*Release Me!*) that felt like a sigh of relief.

Hoisting Kevin in his arms, he sprinted through the Emergency Department doors. He stood cradling the boy in the glaring light as he tried to gain his bearings, the rain puddling from his clothes onto the floor. Under the bright fluorescents the boy's skin had taken on a distinctly greenish hue; he has swallowed my Death Breath, Arty thought as he fought back a surge of anal tremors; I've poisoned him and he's going to die.

Before he could start shouting for help, two nurses came running and the child was plucked from him and put on a gurney. 'What happened?' a doctor was demanding as the trolley wheels squeaked urgently away, the sound covering the swoosh of heavy blats that fell out of Arty. 'Sir? What happened?'

What *happened*? My sin has no more room and it is coming out the only way it knows how – coming out for the world to smell and the good Lord to judge.

'I...I...,' stammered Arty, as a cloud of vapour gushed from him with the reek of diseased carrion. 'His mother's in the car,' said Arty, pulling the doctor away from the blast site, 'you've got to help her too.' The doctor's face knuckled up as he caught a whiff, then he hurried off in the direction of the hapless Lynda, calling for two porters to help him.

Arty's butt was bubbling noisily again. He moved further down the corridor, sounding like a man tramping on ducks, as much to escape his own stench as to avoid the attention of the two cops attending a drunk with a black eye by the coffee machine.

He heard Lynda before he saw her; she was being held upright by the two porters, sobbing maniacally, saying Kevin's name over and over, but at least she was conscious. She raised her flooded eyes and saw him, her face twisting into a Gorgon mask of hate.

'It was him!' she squealed, pointing a trembling finger directly at his heart: '*Him!*'

Arty let out a doleful honk as the two cops abruptly lost interest in the drunk's philosophy lecture and moved toward the hysterical Lynda. 'He tried to kill us!' she was screaming now, 'he tried to –'

Her words were lost as his buttocks warmed to a 21-gun salute. He turned on his heels and fled, hearing the cops' heavy steps echo down the corridor after him. He made it to the elevators just as the doors were closing – he had time to get in, but the thought of getting trapped in there with his own filth made him swing a hard left and make for the stairs instead.

Each frantic step caused him to break wind; he could hear his pursuers lose pace as they coughed and gagged below him. He pushed on through a set of doors, trumping his way through Urology, before running across (*Release Me!*) a corridor link to another building, the rain battering on the windows so hard he felt he was being chased by a horde of armoured marauders.

As he ran, he unleashed a furious onslaught of gas that assailed the eyes as well as the nose. It billowed out behind him like a heat haze; when he chanced a peek over his shoulder, he saw one of the officers on his knees, retching violently.

He burst through a set of double doors, running pell-mell past a man clutching a bouquet of flowers that wilted in his slipstream. He sped on through ward after ward of drained women, each one clutching a pink mewling baby; the infants' cries grew more fevered at his passing.

Christ, he thought, I'm in (*Release Me!*) Maternity. He came to a dead end at the Delivery Suite. He spun around to find the two policemen approaching him slowly with their hands over their mouths.

'Take it easy, sir,' one was saying, his voice muffled by his fingers: 'lie down on the floor and place your hands on the back of your head.'

Quivering screams sprinkled the air and, behind him, in the Delivery Suite a woman swore with hearty gusto to each exhortation to 'Push, push!' Artie took that advice to heart and pushed as hard as he could.

Blowing a hard six on the rectum scale, he strained until something popped in his nose and star spangles danced across his vision. Something within him gave way as his entrails turned to dust and his body sank in on itself like a collapsing dirigible. As the gas enveloped him he saw a malevolent brown eye glaring at him from its nebulous midst and heard a voice (*RELEASE*) mingle with the cries of the policemen (*ME!*) and the exultant yell of 'You're crowning!' from the Delivery Room. Then Arty slumped to the floor in a smoking desiccated heap.

The gas cloud took form briefly; a triumphant amorphous figure punching the air, before dissipating and slinking away under its own fetid steam. It wafted under the doors of the Delivery Suite, funnelling itself down the gullet of the infant taking its first sob spiked gulps of air.

The baby choked and spluttered on it, turning a violent shade of purple as the midwife gave it a smack across the bow; the child retaliated with a cacophonous fart that tapered off into a series of desultory puffs.

'You've got a feisty one here,' laughed the midwife, handing the babe to its beleaguered mother. 'Better out than in I always say; good for the heart you know.'

A. Henry Keene and James Ward Kirk

Exquisite Corpse

1.

The woman's hips moved to the pounding bass from the speakers like a snake moving across a hot desert highway. She wore a blue dress, dark blue, as mother wore. Normally David ignored desperate women, whose need darkened the sweat on their brows and made them grovel at the end of his penis, but this one with the mice swirling around her ankles like debris around a tornado caught his attention.

When David was a child of nine, his mother, wearing one of her countless blue dresses, found a mouse and her litter in a seldom-used closet. David watched her pick up the pups and squeeze each one until the flesh burst. The pink and red guts spewed across her manicured fingernails.

She can be saved, the woman with the mice. He looked at his gold Rolex. *There's still time; her infestation is manageable, and she may be of use.*

His approach was classic; brief eye contact from across the dance floor followed by the saunter. The hunter and the willing prey played the timeless game. He felt the endorphin-rich blood flow through his veins to bring strength to his heart and vigor to his limbs His focus narrowed to the woman and her luscious curves. He wanted desperately to squeeze her.

2.

She felt the chemical reactions of attraction. Her mind filled with hazy visions and vague hallucinations of mystical wholeness, as her body became soft and pliant, and her senses heightened to their utmost. She felt every heartbeat, every brush of fabric, every soft breath that passed her moist lips, and his warm palm upon her cheek. She moistened, and wondered if the man scented her.

"My name is Mary." She sighed. "I noticed you noticing me. I knew it was just a matter of time. It always is." She lit a cigarette, inhaled and exhaled through her nostrils.

"David." He breathed through his mouth, preferring to taste the woman than grieve her aroma. "Mary, there's still time for you."

"Are you my savior?"

"Perhaps." He smiled at Mary. His teeth glowed white in the club light.

"And how will you save me?" She drank from her glass of red wine, and then flavored the sensory input with a final draw from her cigarette. Smoke embellished her hair, adding silver to black.

"I am a thanatologist."

Mary, blushing, took a drag from her cigarette.

"I study death, Mary. Think about it. What happens when we die? The number two best represents the human body. The brain has two hemispheres. We have two lungs, two kidneys. The liver has two halves. The human heart has four chambers, devisable by two. Humans hold within themselves two energies: good and evil. What happens to that coupling of good and evil upon death? I propose that at death good and evil separate. But what happens then?"

David lit his own cigarette. "I'm not speaking the language of seduction. I'm sorry."

"Death. Seduction. They're two basic drives. We seek them in equal measure. They serve similar purposes and function in similar ways. Where death is a parting of pairs, seduction is a pairing of parts." Mary laughed. "You think you can save me? That you can see death upon me, and smell its stench? Well I believe you can. What is the price you charge? You didn't get that expensive watch doing charity work." Mary smirked. "I bet there are a lot of freaks that would love a girl like me. And I bet you're the guy they go to."

David looked about the crowded room. The vermin were multiplying. "I have a place in the countryside, a forty-five minute drive. I can show you . . . secrets."

"Let's go."

3.

"You may not believe this, Mary. But I have invented a machine . . ." David hesitated, rubbed his cheek. *Dare I say? Yes. She is mine to squeeze.*

"Go on. A machine?" Mary prompted.

"Yes. It . . . Well, it captures the good, and the evil as they separate, captures the energy at the moment of death." David

39

looked at Mary. "I believe I can cycle the energy back around to . . ." David laughed. "Well, the machine, if it is set up properly, will cycle the good and evil energies around in such a manner as to harmonize their frequencies and reanimate the body. One becomes healthier than ever and in symphony with life."

"And if it is not set up properly?"

"I guess it wouldn't bring you back."

"Could it bring me back imbalanced?"

"You mean pure evil?" David laughed. "According to my theory of twos, that should not be possible."

"But that is just a theory."

"True."

4.

The two-story house stood in an open field. The crescent moon illuminated a few details: spires at the corners, several crumbling chimneys, floor to ceiling windows. A crack in the foundation was apparent, running from the cellar to just below one of the chimneys.

David helped Mary out of the car. Mice scurried alongside, as they approached the door.

"Are you sure you want to do this?" David opened the door, and pretended not to notice the cockroaches as they scattered.

Mary said, "There's something you need to know. I have a secret."

David, his mind beset by a torrent of contradictory thoughts, led Mary by the hand across the creaking, warped floor of the foyer to the left. They entered the library, lit only by moonlight through the large windows.

He seated her in an over-stuffed leather chair the color of coffee. "Mary, may I offer you a drink?"

"No. But perhaps you should."

David poured a brandy, discreetly glancing at the dark, shifting form of the apparition in the corner of the library. He felt its heavy presence, heard it mumbling with many voices. The rats, too, felt the disturbed presence, scurried from the corner, and set about chewing the walls and floorboards.

David pressed his eyes together tightly for a long moment. He returned to Mary and sat across from her. He crossed his legs, sipped again from his brandy, and asked, "Please tell me your secret."

"The 'good' you speak of that resides in every human being, does not reside within me." She paused for affect. "I am a killer. My first murder was my fraternal twin named Oscar. We were five years old, and it was Christmas Eve. I entered his bedroom and smothered him with his pillow. Oscar was weak, pathetically puny. I think in a way I murdered him in the womb, stole his will to live somehow.

"I wanted his Christmas presents. Nothing more and I got them. 'Poor little Mary' my parents said.

"I did not grieve the loss of Oscar.

"Over the years I have murdered countless people; mostly vagrants and worthless types, but some decent people, like Oscar, who's only flaw was his failure to thrive."

David nodded his head thoughtfully. Inwardly, he was elated; the extreme lack of polarity in her soul made her perfect for his true purpose. Yes, he had the machine. Yes, if properly calibrated, it could reanimate the dead. However, it certainly wasn't calibrated to harmonize energies, as he had long ago lost interest in reanimation.

"Mary." David finished his brandy. "I am not worried about your misdeeds." David watched the mice scurry into Mary's hair and noticed her struggling to breathe. "You have what I need; the strength to finally be one or the other." David reached for an ornate black onyx box. He gingerly removed a scarlet cloth and passed it to Mary. "Breathe deeply. This is the first modest step."

Mary did as requested without hesitation, and her heartbeat grew erratic and weak and her head began to nod.

"My family has lived in this house for generations. Well, actually this is the second house on this spot. When my great, great grandfather Roderick, lived in the original house, the whole thing split in two and sank into the swampy land beneath." David's eye twitched and he licked his lips. "Roderick was convinced that the original house was alive." David rubbed his forehead. "I believe it was, and this house, the second house, it is alive as well. But it is quickly being destroyed by the vermin and--."

David twitched. He jerked his head to the side, as a large chunk of plaster fell from the ceiling.

Mary's head fell to the side and the mice ate into her skull.

"It's time, Mary." David took Mary by the arm.

"Yes, David." Mary whispered.

David lifted Mary from her chair. Mary tried to resist but faintness had overcome her. David carried her limp body down the stone stairs. Her feet skidded across each step and thumped onto the next. When he had reached the bottom, David dragged Mary into his workshop. He stripped off her clothes, strapped her onto a large wooden table, and attached electrodes about her chest and head.

Mary breathed heavily. Leather restraints pressed into her flesh. Sparks flew, as David hurried to adjust some settings on a control panel and disconnect a few wires from the spiral filaments above the table. He jammed the bare wires into the back of his neck at the end of his spine and waited.

The dark form shrieked with several voices from the corner. The house shuddered and groaned.

Mary drew a few sharp breathes.

Her heart stopped.

Gradually the spiral filaments began to glow. Sparks jumped from point to point on the apparatus and Mary's pure dark energy flowed into David's nervous system.

David's body shook.

The shadowy figure produced a multiplicity of screams, which, as David's body and mind was overwhelmed by Mary's energy, condensed into the mad snarl of a single voice.

David fell to the rough stone floor. He was dead for a moment. When his heart resumed beating, it did so with greater gusto than ever before.

David removed the electrodes and stood before his unwitting benefactor. Mary's flesh was ashen. Her face expressed an ease and comfort that was lacking during her tormented life.

David, with rough, powerful movements, disconnected the electrodes and removed the leather straps that held Mary tight upon the table. He moved onto the table, began stomping Mary's middle, and did not stop until her eyes burst outward and her guts squished beneath his feet.

Exhausted and complete, he dragged her depleted body to a large fireplace, doused it with gasoline, and set it alight.

David watched her flesh burn with single-minded attention. He smiled.

On the open field, the house loomed large and foreboding. Dark smoke wafted from the chimney.

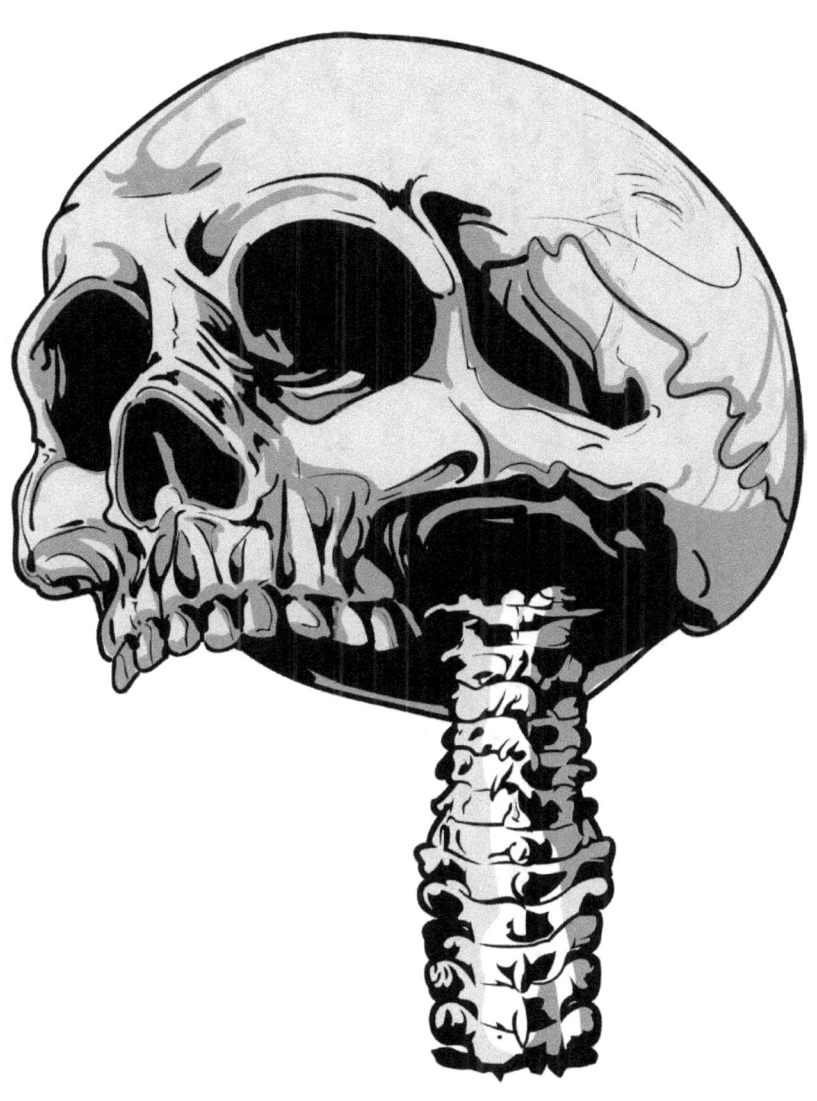

Keep going—It only gets weirder!

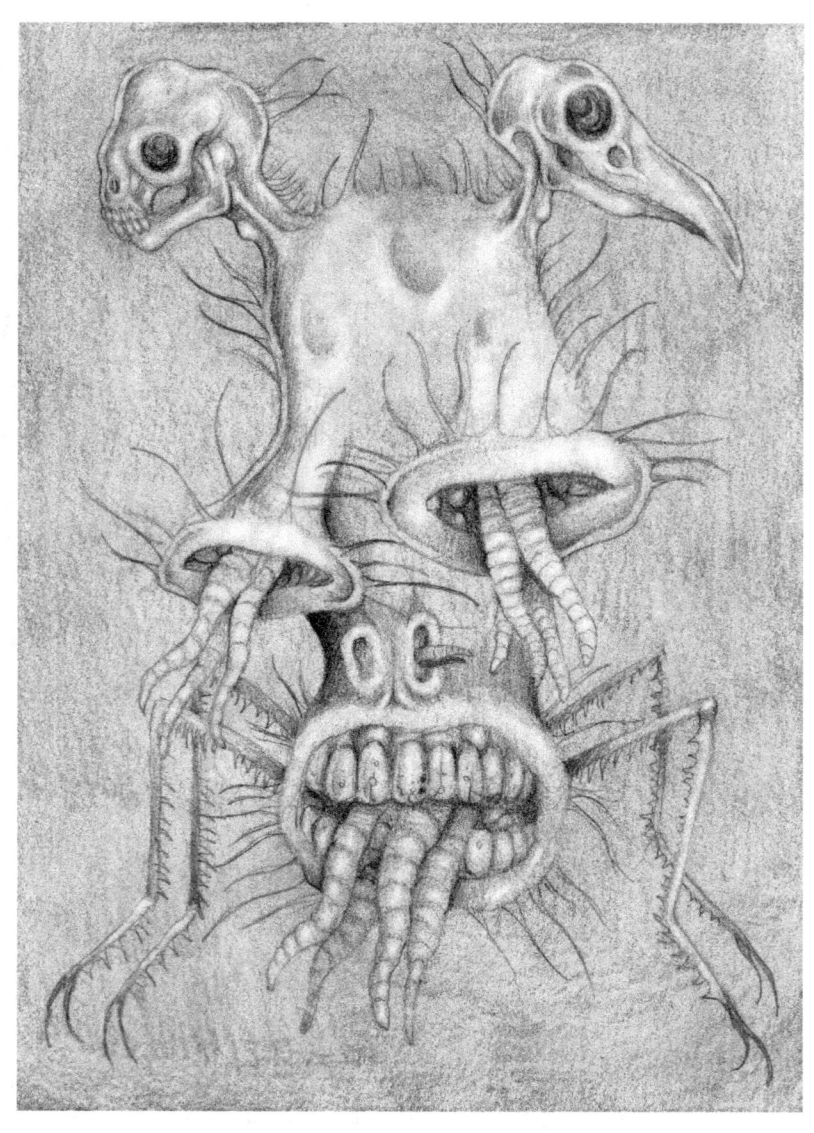

William Cook

The Receiver

I received the call yesterday. My mother has died of cancer. The Big C. My world is collapsing in graduating seconds; each tick of the clock seems less regulated by the laws of physics. I have retreated to my safe place. My panic room bunker. My eyes closed last night but I fear that sleep has escaped me now, forever. All that remains is the grim cold reality of a world dipped in death.

The phone continues to ring, incessantly.

ddddddaaannnnngggg   *ddddddaaannnnngggg ddddddaaannnnngggg*

Each trilling tone grows louder.

ddddddaaannnnngggg   *Ddddddaaannnnngggg DDDDDDAAAANNNNNGGGG*

The noise ascends, demanding to be heard.

DDDDDDAAANNNNNGGGG   *DDDDDDAAANNNNNGGGG DDDDDDAAANNNNNGGGG*

The concrete room is rectangular – the walls painted a dirty white – a single fluorescent tube buzzes and pops overhead intermittently, the sound – like kamikaze flies frying on an electric bug catcher. At the far end of the room, the phone (old style bell red) vibrates with a shrill sonar, sitting on a small hardwood desk.

DDDDDDAAANNNNNGGGG

DDDDDDAAANNNNNGGGG

DDDDDDAAANNNNNGGGG

I slowly walk towards the desk, my hearing collapses beneath the wall of sound. All I hear, rather – feel, are my own footfalls. At first, light clicking taps, then . . . leaden sonic booms:

TAP, CLICK, TAP, CLICK, TAP, THUD, THUD, THUMP, THUD, THUMP, THUMP, BOOM, THUMP, BOOM, BOOM, BOOM . . .

A white cloaked arm reaches out before me. I notice the flesh on my hand glistens; colored black like obsidian. My fingers look like talons, unbendable, immobile, but yet they extend and stretch until they close about the red plastic receiver and lift the handset to my waiting ear. A burst of static and the fluorescent light flickers frenetically above me. A strobe light – the white-hot light burns. The intense vision has a sound that can only be seen . . .

WAH WAH WAH WAH WAH WAH WAH WAH WAH WAH WAH WAH WAH WAH WAH WAH

And then the light strobes slowly to one color . . .

FLIP FLIP FLIP FLIP FLIP FLIP FLIP . . .

. . . to a low burning point overhead – a slight blue tinge surrounds the dim length of tube, now cold and sombre but with still enough light to cast a shadow down onto the off-white concrete floor. I see the black shape of me – elongated, shadowed, the looping coils of the telephone receiver cable, twisting and turning up my arm like a serpentine demon. I detect a sound, coming from far away down the telephone line. My breath clouds before me like steam, but thicker, like exhaust fumes or ectoplasm.

I shiver as the faint sound graduates in pitch.

My hand is vibrating now and the room has grown frigid as an ice-locker. The sharp monotone increases in volume and pitch, to the point where it is a needle of sound, pushing its sharp point deep into my brain, agonizing fraction by fraction . . . I pick up the hand-set and raise it to my ear.

Somewhere, faintly, in the distance, a phone rings. Somewhere, someone dies. Someone is born, someone is murdered. Somewhere, something is happening, that cannot be explained by reality or words. Death creeps along the telephone line, searching for the right receiver – the sonic intercept, the relay switch that will channel its chilled message deep within the receptor's mind. Searching for the pinprick of light buried deep within the blackness of the soul – whereby it might escape into the lost minutia of the cosmic apocalypse . . .

I drop the handset. It clatters to the concrete floor, the red plastic casing shatters into fragments only to liquefy, just as suddenly, into splattered pools of glistening maroon. The dim light from above now casts a leukemic glow, like an aura, down below on the phone fragments. The concave edge of the sickly light swells and slowly creeps across the floor, away from the shattered phone and myself. The edge of the light is inky black, like space. The blood glistens mercurially as the fluorescent above suddenly flickers erratically and then settles into a bright white light, once again.

I listen to the electrical hum and let my eyes readjust to the brightness enveloping my mind.

I blink until my eyes acclimate to the revealed scene before me. The cold concrete room is as it was before. My breath comes in frigid plumed clouds of condensation. The remnants of the red plastic phone casing, some fragments still solid amongst the bloody liquefied pools, vibrate and clatter on the cement floor like epileptic crabs before melting into bloody globule pools. I watch them accelerate towards each other, like plasma-filled marbles or blood-swollen eyeballs, melting into each other at my feet – condensing, morphing, into a shape. A human shape. First the bulbous torso, slick blood glazed plasticity, bubbling and swelling as first a limb and then another, then another and another and then, finally, another bursts from the main core.

A head appears like a mannequin, smooth and slick with viscos fluid, as it erupts from the swollen torso; transforming, until features begin to define and mold themselves to its features as it begins to resemble something vaguely, but unmistakeably, human. The misshapen torso and long thin limbs rearrange until it is an obviously female form.

A phone begins to ring in the distance.

I look up. The room stretches away from me. At the end of the room against the dirty white wall, now flecked and splattered with arcs of blood, on the small hardwood table sits another phone. Black, shiny plastic – much-like the obsidian claw that extends out from the white arm of my lab-coat.

The phone now rings incessantly.

dddddaaannnnngggg   dddddaaannnnngggg dddddaaannnnngggg

I walk towards it. Each trilling tone grows louder. More intense.

dddddaaannnnngggg   Dddddaaannnnngggg DDDDDDAAANNNNNGGGG

he noise ascends, like a frenetic fire alarm, as I approach.

DDDDDDAAANNNNNGGGG   DDDDDDAAANNNNNGGGG DDDDDDAAANNNNNGGGG

I increase my speed as I walk towards the desk, my hearing collapsing beneath the sound again. My footsteps add to the cacophony of sound as my sense of urgency balloons. I. Must. Answer. The. Phone . . .

DDDAAANNNNNGGGG,   TAP,   CLICK,   TAP, DDDAAANNNNNGGGG,   CLICK,   TAP,   THUD,

DDDAAANNNNNGGGG,	*THUD,*	*THUMP,*
DDDAAANNNNNGGGG,	*THUD,*	*THUMP,*
DDDAAANNNNNGGGG,	*THUMP,*	*BOOM,*
DDDAAANNNNNGGGG,	*THUMP,*	*BOOM,*
DDDAAANNNNNGGGG,	*BOOM, BOOM*	*. . .*
DDDAAANNNNNGGGG . . .		

I pick it up.

SSSSSSSSSSSSSSSonnnnnnnnnnnnnnnnnnnnnnnnnnnnnn . . ."

It is my mother's voice. The voice of a serpent.

*"Yyyoooooooouuuuuuu   mmmmmuuusssssstttttt
ddddddddiiiiiiiiieeeeeeeeeeeeeeee . . ."*

I drop the handset and it explodes into a shattered jigsaw of plastic and components across the concrete floor. I stumble back against the table, steadying myself with my blackened hands as I gulp air down deep into my icy lungs. I look back down the room in the opposite direction. The bloodied form is now moving, peeling itself from the ground. With each passing second its form gains density, definition, and now it walks with a lilting gait. Each step followed by a more definitive approach, more self-assured, as it lopes my way. A scream escapes from between my clenched teeth as I watch it evolve into its final form. I hold onto the table as the room tilts and my legs collapse beneath me. The corners of my vision fill with a brilliant phosphorescent light as the shape reaches out to me. Her form expands and fills my vision, the all-encompassing darkness of her evil pixelates with the intense white light. The stabbing pin of sound instantly intensifies inside my cranium to crescendo pitch, as I realize that I am the receiver.

I am the pinprick of light, buried deep within the blackness of the soul. My soul! And it is my mother, who now stands before me, gushing streams of light flowing from her abyssal eyes, twisting like tornadoes of electricity as the light merges and bursts forth into my consciousness. Penetrating every pore, every atom of my being, as I become the darkness. The last sound I hear is the distant ringing of a telephone, fading into the distance with each subsiding trill – eternally calling, waiting for another receiver. Another means by which its message can be relayed.

Jaap Boekestein

Fair Chance

Maybe what I do is wrong. No, scrap that, what I do is *definitely* wrong. Morally wrong, ethically wrong, fucking insane actually. I am aware of that. I *know*. At least I give them a chance. I gave all six of them a chance. It is more than I ever got.

Yes, they died and I am alive. I would not be telling this tale now if I was dead, would I? I gave them a chance, and a shot to *feel* something.

To *feel*.

I know.

Yes, I know. Just because I like it does not mean everyone else likes it. I suspect most, if not all, do not like to feel. Maybe you only like it when you survive; maybe I am the exception to the rule. I am sure there are others out there who think and feel the same as I - who would come running to me if they knew what I have to offer.

I am sure of it.

Earl did not like guns.

"Home protection," some of the people said when they discussed firearms. "The Second Amendment!"

"I just don't like guns," would be his response. "I don't like someone having a weapon in their hands that can kill me as easily as swatting a fly. No easier."

"So get a gun yourself. Protect yourself."

Earl would laugh when they said that. Because some people had guns, then everyone needed to have a gun? Where was the free choice in that? He didn't use that argument anymore. He knew from experience it would not convince anyone. It just wasn't worth the energy.

So when he got burgled he could not chase the guy away. Because he did not own a gun.

Neither did the burglar, actually. The dope head who broke in Earl's house was armed with just a knife. Unfortunately, Earl was at home.

There was a fight.

The junkie was a wiry guy, no muscles, no fat. He was destroying his body slowly, shot by shot. His brains were already gone for the most part.

Now Earl was a big man. True, it was mostly fat, but compared to the dope head he was Arnold fucking Schwarzenegger. The burglar was high on something. Earl didn't know if it was meth or heroin. He only knew that he kept punching the wiry guy and the guy would not go down.

Earl slipped at one point, and by accident pulled the other guys pants down. In retrospect, he thought that was funny.

While the burglar pulled up his pants, Earl rose to his feet. At that point, Earl discovered he was bleeding. He had a cut to his skull, another crossing his cheek and a third on his throat that missed his jugular by less than an inch.

The wiry guy had a knife in his hand.

In the heat of the fight, Earl had not noticed the weapon before, or felt the cuts. That can happen.

Now Earl knew the guy had a knife.

From that point, Earl did not think, he just *did*.

In a rush, Earl stormed the guy, wrestled him and twisted the guy's arm.

The knife went into the burglar's chest, piercing his heart.

This time the burglar dropped.

Earl managed to call 911 before passing out from blood loss.

He came to in the hospital, unable to talk. The surgeons inserted a plastic tube in Earl's trachea, to prevent his throat from swelling and suffocating him. The tube came out a few days later, which was a pretty terrible experience in and of itself: holding your breath while someone pulls out the damn thing. Pulling the catheter out of his penis was no picnic either, but that trach tube... Damn, that was really nasty.

In the meantime, Earl learned the burglar was dead.

Somehow, that was an enormous comfort to Earl. The fucker was dead.

In a week's time, Earl was released from hospital. The doctors discussed plastic surgery but Earl wanted nothing to do with it.

"I've been in hospital once because of that bastard. I'm not going in a second time because of him."

Secretly Earl was even a bit proud of his scars. *Warrior's scars,* he called them. Someone did this to me and I survived. I fucking damn well survived. You can see it in my face. I survived.

Earl did counseling, he talked to a shrink, he talked to a support group, he did therapy - the whole nine yards. It was all a bit redundant since he felt no trauma, had no nightmares, nor was he afraid. The bastard was dead, and he survived. It was a simple as that.

Or maybe not...

There was one little problem.

One tiny little thing that made Earl pause and think.

When he thought about the fight he felt... well, a bit excited. No, actually more then just a bit. He felt very excited. Muchos excited.

Earl remembered exactly how the fight made him feel. He remembered it all.

He felt alive during the fight.

Alive as he had never felt before.

And damn, that was a nice feeling.

Okay, it is not sexual. It wasn't with the four guys and it wasn't with the two girls. I don't get off on them. I don't do things with them while they're alive and I sure as hell don't do anything with them after they're dead, except, of course, disposing the body. By all definitions, I'm a psychopath and I don't want to be caught. Neither imprisonment nor the death penalty appeals to me. I am probably insane, but not that insane. I am sanely insane.

That was a joke, by the way.

Sorry, it was not a very good joke, but screw it. I'm alone and I'm laughing.

Anyway, it's not sexual. Hell no. It is something stronger, something finer. A fight to the death. You know only one will survive and he – or she – knows that too. I am very clear to let them know what will happen and what their chances are. I have a knife, they have knife. I will try to kill them and the only way they are getting out alive, is if they kill me.

So far, all six failed.

Three tried and fought back. Three did not. They chose to cry and beg. Even after I started stabbing and cutting them.

I pitied them, but still I killed them. They could not accept my gift to *feel*. The primeval rush to kill or be killed. To be predator or prey.

The other three accepted my gift and gave me all they had. It was wonderful.

As I said, I survived, but some of them managed to inflict their share of damage. I have the scars to prove it. I'm proud of them. When I'm alone in bed, I sometimes touch them; caress them, while reliving the fights.

Oh, did only the women beg and the men fight?

One woman and two men chose to fight, the other woman and two of the men begged. I don't think it's a gender thing. Some people will fight; some people will try to flee. It is just who they are. I give them a fair chance to discover who they are and to survive the whole thing by killing me. It is insane, but then, so am I.

Earl started working out. Not because he wanted to lose some of his fat. No, because... well, you know... "I will able to defend myself," he told others.

Deep down he knew that was not the reason, but Earl would not admit that. Not even to his self.

He tried kendo first. Some introductory lessons. The samurai in the movies always looked so damned cool, like Uma Thurman in *Kill Bill*. Yeah, wielding a katana was fucking great.

It wasn't. Too many rules and too little of the rush he craved. Just short bursts where the opponents try to hit each other with a wooden sword. No, that wasn't what he wanted. He needed something more physical, more primitive. He needed to get down to the level of sweating and grunting – flesh against flesh.

He tried boxing next. For a time that seemed to do the trick, but only for a while. Again, rules. Again, no rush. Not really. You could never really let go.

Earl kept searching. Taekwondo, krav maga, cage fighting, et al. They were all fine, they were all great, in the end they all failed to fulfill Earl's craving.

One night, Earl came close to recapturing the feeling he was seeking. It was in a parking lot outside a bar. He had words with a guy inside the drinking establishment. Outside, they beat the crap out of each other. All those martial arts lessons paid off, the other guy ended up down and out on the ground, leaving Earl standing, panting, and sweating. In that brief moment, Earl had felt it. He had felt *alive*. He had really fucking felt *alive*. It was the other guy or him. Simple. No rules, no mercy. It was that whole Fight Club thing.

Somehow it still was not enough.

Back home, while taking a hot shower, Earl realized why it was not enough.

It had been close and during the fight, he had really felt it, but afterward... There was only an empty feeling. A little bit of shame even. No joy of winning. No joy of survi...

Earl stopped breathing, not finishing that thought. Not daring to finish. Still, his mind did: *surviving*.

There was no joy of surviving. Not in the same way he felt after beating the dope head. Fighting, just fighting, was not enough. Winning was not enough. What he was looking for was surviving a potentially fatal contest. Man to man; two enter, one leaves. Kill or be killed.

Earl threw up in the toilet.

He sat in the shower and cried.

He felt sick, he felt dirty.

The knives are the same. The arena is my basement, carefully adjusted: well lit, soundproofed, no exits except for the heavy locked door. The key is in my pocket. I always explain these things carefully before I cut them loose. They can pick up the knife. I am waiting on the other side of the room, near the door, armed with the other knife.

When they pick up the knife, the battle starts. If they don't pick up the knife, I take the initiative. Some need a little convincing that this really is a fight to the death. But that never takes long. If you see a scarred maniac with a knife coming for you, your instincts take over. Sadly, some try to flee, but others opt to fight.

Now selecting opponents is the part I actually hate. You would think that selecting them, following him, luring him (or her), seducing her (or him), getting them drunk or whatever method is employed, would be exciting. Doubtless, for some psychopaths it is. But not for me. It makes me nervous as hell and I always feel sick from fear of discovery.

A knife evens out the odds a little bit, but still I don't chose weaklings, the crippled, or the puny. I'm a pretty big guy; they must have a fair chance. Even with the women, I only select those who I think will give me a run for my money.

Yeah I know I am crazy, but I mean what I say: they must have a fair chance. The fight really needs to be about life and death. Theirs and mine.

I find them in bars; I find them in streets, in parking lots, even in parks. Four I have grabbed, but that is difficult and risky. They struggle, try to escape. Several *have* managed to get away. That was bad. It was dangerous but that's not the kind of danger I want.

Two of them I chatted up, one in a bar and one in a parking lot. Those were easier, but riskier in a way. There are cameras everywhere nowadays.

I am not sure how I'll get the next one. Maybe abduct them from their house?

Now, that is a thought.

I have to think about that, but it absolutely has potential. Just find someone living alone. Get in, snatch them and get out. Hm... Of course I would need to park close by, and no nosy neighbors, but it could work. It could definitely work.

"Make me feel like you are going to kill me," Earl asked the woman. "Tie me up, beat me, strangle me, I don't care. Make me feel you will kill me. I need to feel."

The professional dominatrix nodded. This was by far the weirdest request she had ever got. Some people had really strange needs but she felt it was something she could provide, she could bring them to that place they needed to be.

She tied Earl up, she beat him, she used needles and a knife. The knife was mostly for the mind-fuck: just a lot of scratching on his body and putting the point of the knife just under his eyes, on his tongue and under his chin. That got a strong response: tears, a whole flood. Apparently, though, it was not enough, because he kept begging: "Kill me. Kill me."

So she put a plastic bag on his head.

The see through plastic bag stuck to his wet cheeks. He sucked up the air and did not move. She watched him carefully; most people went berserk at this stage, but not this guy. He seemed to welcome the danger. God created some strange customers, but he loved them all.

At the very last moment, just before he went out, she cut the plastic near his mouth.

Earl sucked up the air. He felt dizzy, he felt like floating. It was a nice feeling, but it was not enough.

He survived, but it was all fake. It was not enough.

Disappointed, he thanked the woman afterward. It was not her fault it had not worked out the way he'd hoped.

Earl drove home. What the hell was he going to do?

I have selected a guy. He lives alone, at the end of a lane. Secluded. Perfect.

I have broken into his house and I'm waiting. I hear his car in the driveway.

I am excited. I will give him my gift, a chance to feel.

There was a key in the dead man's pockets, just as he had said.

Earl opened the door and looked back. The sandy floor was soaking up the blood.

Sick fuck.

The guy was very dead, but strangely, he looked happy.

Sick fuck. Earl did not move. He looked at the basement; he remembered what the guy had told him, just before the fight. The gift. Surviving. The feeling.

Sick fuck.

...

I understand.

I survived, it feels good.

Fucking great.

Earl went up the stairs. He needed to call the cops, he...

He stopped again, looking back.

Sick, sick fuck.

This time he was not talking to the corpse.

Donald Armfield
:: Owl in the Box ::

Chop, chop, apace!
      Box in the owl

I will use its nightly vision
      over this nightmare, a restless dream

A sudden blink of terror
      closes my eyes again
          and the owl in the box

It started with darkness
      and someone yelling

WAKE UP!   WAKE UP!

Then the mist settled in
      and I lost my way
          but found the voice

Chop, chop, apace!
      Box in the owl

Eventually, I won't fail
      and capture the owl

awake to where it all starts
      or was there always.....
          darkness, a restless dream?

Chop, chop, apace!
      Box in the owl

Donald Armfield
When do I awake?

They're out there,
I can feel them
hear their footsteps....
shh!

Disguising their true form.
As dark shadows
along the walls.
They stop
& stare.

I always rush inside,
right before they take
a third step.
Just wait with me.....
Let them
pass through us,
please?

I have a feeling
that's what
they wanna do.
I need to see this....
So I can finally wake up.

Eric LaRocca

Homebody

"You may move now, Zelda," he grunted, turning from her and cupping his wilting erection with both hands.

The size of Francis Bishop's generosity was not to be underestimated when he was taking care of her. After all, minding her health was an important responsibility during the activity. She demanded very little when participating in these forced sexual exercises of complete immobility; her concentration unmoved by any polite inquiry he would pant in her ear concerning well-being.

Zelda often wondered, however, if he ever saw her wince, lamenting in the banality, or if he ever recognized the indifference in her eyes while she laid her on her backside, thighs stiffened together with feet pointed to the ceiling, and ass ornamented with a velvet cushion to imitate a chair.

Then again, Zelda saw how he was often too distracted with the growing between his legs, his bloodless pink second head suddenly inflating purple and impatient to be dismissed with temporary easement. Regardless, whether she was on all fours, head bowed, mouth gagged, and spine flattened to accommodate a panel of wood where he would rest candles and books, or whether he had sent her to face a corner in their one bedroom apartment, her face – her naked body's only secret – hidden by a lampshade, Zelda recognized Francis had looked after her like no other man had before. Not even her father.

Regardless, something had changed in his temperament. Although he had once insisted that their exercises be sanctified by the token of a lick of appreciation, the ceremony was often left without consummation, but rather an embarrassment or a dissatisfaction that would remain festering until it could possibly be absolved the next time. Zelda had once recognized a mischievous enchantment warming in his disposition as the separation of motionlessness was disengaged. They would flinch wildly as if reveling in otherworldly orgasms while their bodies met after the prolonged absence and her sprawling pink muscle would flex itself across his cheeks with doggish reverence.

Her post-sex adulation was plainly no longer appreciated as she watched him shudder at the mere suggestion of her touch or, more commonly, rushed to the washroom avoiding any further remark. Of course, Zelda had more than anticipated the eventual tiresome nature of marital obligations. After all, she recalled the recognition of her mother's uncaring and dispirited nature after the age of sixty towards her father.

However, she hadn't expected this uninterested nature towards eroticism to prosper in their bed after merely eighteen months of marriage. She had to concede her unconventional venereal circumstance played a significant role in their compromise.

It was after a seventy-minute session of stillness that Francis startled Zelda by gesturing for her to join him on the bed. She had been standing where two of the four walls without pictures or paintings met, arms at both of her sides, hands cupping her freshly shaven groin, and head secreted by a square lampshade. His tired gesture and unhurried shambling indicated a private defeat.

"I c-can't pretend to know w-why you're s-so glum," Zelda stammered, her usual nervousness thickening and her tone as light as the muffled drone of downtown Hartford, Connecticut outside.

Then again, she was reminded with a hint as the hairless pearl between her thighs itched at the memory of the admitted pointlessness of last night's razor. She wondered why she had shaven in the first place. She knew full well Francis wouldn't be able to use it anyhow.

That's what every gynecologist and venereal specialist in New England had cautioned her and her parents after a routine physical following her eighteenth birthday. She couldn't believe eight years had passed since she underwent a two week inspection once she had confessed to her pediatrician her loins had never been baptized by the traditional redness of womanhood.

"God knows I've d-done everything y-you've asked of me and more."

The white wool sweater she had slipped on was beginning to chafe as it beaded diamonds of sweat from her softening teats; they, too, exhausted of all readiness.

She saw his eyes lower, an uneasiness broiling in his temperament as though any words might separate the fetter between he and she already tethered by the most tenuous of truces.

He nodded, agreeing. "Yes. You have."

She watched how careful he was to keep his face out of the light, eyes avoiding her at all costs, presumably embarrassed by his face's only discernable fault in the shape of a reddish birthmark that stretched from the left side of his chin to his left temple.

"I thought you were – s-satisfied. Y-y-you said it was what you w-wanted. You know I would train my body to do anything for you," she said, cupping her hands together as if straining to offer a final donation of her body from the nothingness in her palm. "B-but, you know there are certain things that my body can't - do no m-matter how determined I am or – h-how strong your conviction."

Francis was not without answers, however; as finely lubricated as they were, they lilted with their polished harmlessness and yet she saw his deliberate urgency as he teased his tongue between the gap in his front teeth. "Surely there are more specialists we could see. You said the one in Farmington had told you the benefits of dilation treatment. There are more options."

"People with m-m-money have options. We - don't," she reminded.

Zelda thought of her parents and the uncertainty of whether or not the landlord would knock on their door, the clothes that were often two sizes too small or stained beyond the point of mending from previous owners, and her mother's purple eye after her father had learned she had spent a week's paycheck on Zelda's ballet lessons.

"Th-they said it would be wrong to reject what God had given me," Zelda said. "In fact, they said it w-was better this w-way. A girl gets used to being s-spoiled by men, they said. M-m-makes her less of a woman."

Even if her mother's admonition of the lessening of a woman through physical pleasure were true, Zelda would welcome it unabashed as she knew full well that the traditional rites of womanhood were forever lost to her. Her mother, seemingly happy with perverted wisdom, had convinced her that no man would ever accept a wife not fully a woman and likely to grow impatient and seek out other means of amusement.

She couldn't help but remember her eleven-year-old bewilderment at the bloodied cotton tubes tasseled with strings she had seen in the girl's lavatory waste cans after ballet recital. She recalled how that puzzlement had hardened to an unflinching resentment after the age of eighteen of something she could never have. She remembered the shameless curiosity of her pubescent fingers following the region below her pubis, uncovering the small dimple, and expecting it as a future conduit for pleasure and life force only to have the anticipation dashed at the doctor's truth of what it really was – nothingness, a crude imitation of womanhood.

"I know things haven't been well since you've been out of work," he said.

"You've k-k-kept me out of – w-work," she reminded him, the sadness in her tone changing to surprise at her sudden brashness. She felt her body stiffen from her countless exercises in exactness that had forever robbed her from the fluidity of her dance where she existed by movement and needed no words. Zelda had often sensed the confines of her body harden from its expert flexibility as balmy, red monsters swollen from rigidity inflamed the entirety of her form.

Despite the structure these exercises may have provided, they were not without their faults, as Francis demanded that she, sometimes, stand naked for ten hours at a time as though she were merely a permanent ornament of the apartment.

"I like to make sure I take care of you," he reminded. Any further sincerity was quieted as he finished, "It doesn't matter anyhow. I'll be due some money from disability soon anyhow."

He cringed as he stood. Zelda guessed his neck must have been paining him again.

"My c-condition never bothered you before," she said.

Francis seemed to have an answer prepared for that as well. "But, talking only gets you so much. I'm talking about basic human hunger. The belly gets hungry. You feed it. Sexual organs get hungry too."

Zelda watched Francis's eyes drift from her to regard the unmade bed - pillows tossed carelessly, sheets unfurled on one side and wrapped on the other.

"You don't even sleep in the bed anymore," he said, head lowering again.

"I t-told you. I c-can't – s-s-sleep on that mattress."

She of course wouldn't tell him about the countless nights her body flinched, sensing tiny nuggets beneath the mattress that not only bulged like wads of flint as though they had been born from the restlessness of every failed conversation and every failed penetration. They squirmed, however, as though answering every one of their movements and, almost, matching the tinder of her restlessness.

Zelda had never told him how many nights she'd strained to stay quiet while her body rocked at the motion of his pelvis reeling against the mattress. Thrust after thrust, until his milky secret had dribbled out, she would shrink, grieved at how easy it was for his appendage to confess the otherwise untold to mere furniture.

"The b-body has m-m-more than one opening, you know." As foolish as she felt saying it, she hoped her frankness somehow might sway him. "You j-just always – sh-shy away from the alternatives."

Zelda suddenly saw his eyes hardening with an intent that she had only earlier seen matched in the front of his trousers. She watched his birthmark twitch, his facial muscles loosening with joy.

"Unless you and I parented a new opening," Francis said, the faintness in his demeanor opposing the stiffening enthusiasm between his legs. "You and I, together, could make a brand new pleasure center for your body. Something that you and I can create and share."

Zelda was without movement. She marveled at how long he must have considered the option in the breadth of those exercises of silence and the impressiveness of his patience at waiting until this very moment. She wondered if he had rehearsed it, if his whispering into the bedding and cushions late at night was his means of privately calculating this very moment.

Francis gripped the pair of shears sitting on the nightstand that Zelda often used to score the soles of her ballet slippers. She saw the cutters suddenly as though they presented so much unseen potential that had never been considered.

"It doesn't have to be a deep one," he promised. "Just enough to allow a – bodily connection. And after the first one heals, we can make another. And then another."

Zelda couldn't help but sense her body fruiting with the prospective of the only children they could possibly parent – genderless siblings of identical inflating valves of motherly tissue bloodied by the same father of metal.

"It will make you feel like a real woman," he added, smiling.

63

Any deafness or disinterest in Zelda's disposition towards his idea was flattened with his words, frantic curiosity visibly sowed in its place. Francis brandished the scissors as though he knew the way well. Her sudden interest could certainly not be mistaken for fright as her lips parted, eyes widening, enraptured by imagining monthly bleedings bubbling in the clefts of her skin raked open by sharpness as a means to endure annual bleedings the way all other women do.

She heaved, convinced it would be then that she would share with other women the practice of abandoning bloodied cloth in waste cans. Most importantly, it would be then that her body would open, leak torrents of red, and be irrigated by molten cream colored broth as a token of reward for the glory of her womanhood.

She said nothing. It was her body that spoke agreement as she shifted her weight onto the center of the bed, pulled off her sweater, moistened her lips, and cupped her left breast. Francis mounted the bed, shears in hand; the red glow of the light on the petite end table beside the bed emphasized the doggedness of his erection, unflinching in its sudden inspiration, as he drew nearer.

She no longer regarded his genitalia with girlish immaturity as though it were merely a small acorn below a nest of sprigs, but rather an instrument toughening with the opportunity of speaking otherwise untold appetites that had been intimidated until now. His whole face arrived in the garish glow of the red light and she saw his birthmark, unchanging burgundy in its flagrant inflammation, harden as though it were greasepaint for battle.

As he squinted, Zelda imagined him searching her face as though straining to memorize the rawness of the moment in its entirety for future recollections in order to persuade some stiffness when these new exercises, too, began to grow tedious in their familiarity. Regardless, the rehearsed mechanicalness of his movements confirmed to Zelda that he had lived this moment time and time again in the confines of his brain.

"Wait–!" he said, mouth opened, and brow furrowed with what seemed to indicate the prospect of a new idea.

He shooed her from the bed, unfurling the comforter and dragging the linens and pillows off. Francis took hold of the naked mattress, heaving its whole body onto the floor. He motioned to it with an embellished gesture as though he were venerating it as a holy altar where the most pleasurable of pleasures and horrible and horrors could be exalted. She saw him look to her, almost insisting some sort of wince of appreciation. She returned him none, however. Only confusion.

"Since it's our first time doing this," he explained, "I wanted it to be – not only special, but - primal." Francis writhed, visibly unable to restrain his excitement. "As though I'd just removed a bone from my rib and made you out of it," he hummed, waving her to the makeshift altar with such friendliness that was entirely dissonant to the unnaturalness of the impending activity.

What little grit of determination Zelda had been clenching behind her tightened lips was drained as Francis pressed his mouth to hers, sucking it out through his permanent smile. All pleasure for her was unraveled, too, as he unknotted the tangles from her hair with his free hand. His body felt entirely new to her as he mounted the bed; he was no longer a disembodied voice without form or meaning, but firming with a language that could only be spoken through the nature of flesh and the dampness of his musk.

Although she already felt Francis's sweaty hardness pressing against her and clapping against her midriff, she couldn't help but notice a peculiar tear in the cushioning of the mattress. The split was only the size of a small polyp and the limits of it were calcified a reddish brown as though a thick syrup had been leaking and had eventually calloused.

Zelda looked back to Francis and saw him smiling.

"You're not scared of it, are you?"

"Wh-what is it?" she asked, cautious to bring her fingers close to the pinkish lips of the bedding's aperture as they dilated impetuously.

"It's grown quite a bit since I first opened it up two weeks ago," he confessed, gently petting the opening.

Zelda noticed how it seemed to temper its enthusiasm, sensitive to the slightest hint of his touch. The opening's immediate physical reaction bore a striking resemblance to the profound flinch of a jellyfish as it, too, operated on the most undeveloped applications of sensory.

"When I first started, it was only the size of a mere pinhole."

"How is - it m-moving–?" Zelda asked, her tenor unsteady with disgust.

Francis said nothing, but cupped his groin in a gesture that signaled to Zelda as though his manhood, inflexible in its unbending excitement, knew the answer and could only disclose the inexpressible through action.

"It's gotten more and more eager."

Zelda recoiled, her nostrils twitching at the damp mustard scent permeating from the orifice. "H-h-how on earth—?"

To her astonishment, with every movement Francis made as he straddled her, the round vent in the mattress widened, hissing a tortured gasp so pitched that it sounded like a soft whistle. The hole, inflating more and more as if emulating the coquettish fervor of a female sex organ anticipating insertion, moistened, oozing what she could imagine as countless sessions of Francis's self-indulgence as it gurgled soft licks of wetness.

"I thought it could join us," he said.

Zelda heaved as she felt the cold frankness of the shears press against her abdominals while she watched his free hand pamper the bloated spigot in the mattress. She scowled for an instant, feeling foolish as she envied all the pleasures she imagined the vent could offer him that she could not. For sudden fear that the hand readying the shears pressing against her stomach might be tempted to follow suit and fully indulge Zelda's competitor, she grabbed hold of Francis's body, bringing his ear to her lips.

"Make me a woman," she heaved, her sudden uninhibitedness hinting her hope that she might sway him from any thought of returning to his second lover.

Francis acquiesced as he tightened his grip about the bow of the scissors, carefully guiding them down the lobes of her breasts, waist, and ending at her left thigh. Although their tip was smart in its pointed astuteness, her flesh inflaming lines of red suggesting where the shears had mapped, she suffocated any apprehension or look of pain, utterly convinced that Francis was about to deliver upon her the rites of true womanhood.

She panted as though her body was readying to mushroom with new life, the small round vent in the mattress whistling like her midwife, and the cradle of the mattress exalting what only man could do and God could not. With one simple fleck of Francis's wrist and the under the encouragement of the serrated edge, her thigh opened up. She thrashed at the glorifying wetness of what she considered to be her rebirth as it magnificently drained a lifetime's denial of bleedings.

Zelda's pleasure was short lived, however, as Francis persuaded the shears in deeper and deeper within the gash. She felt him move the shears up and down the unfolding fluting of her open tendon and muscle, redness jumping in fat spurts with every push.

He made no sound other than childish bleats of glee. She couldn't help but wonder if he might be reveling in the fact that she, too, was now mutilated with a permanent mark like him. With strands of hair glued to her forehead by sweat, Zelda's entire body twitched like a puppet under the duress of every shove of metal. She howled as Francis jerked the shears in a sudden twist, the scissors squelching with a jellied gurgle as they slipped out of her.

"Beautiful, woman," he panted.

She watched as he lovingly admired the ingenuity of the crude imitation of female genitalia he had widened along her thigh, its immaturity presumably now dressed with uncountable opportunities of sexual relief that no mere conventional sex organ could offer. She saw his eyes darting back and forth between the aperture winking along her thigh and the small vent in the bedding, his passion indicating equal admiration in both partners.

Zelda flinched, squealing, as Francis cupped both of his hands around the inflamed lips of her fresh opening. It winked, inflating under the pressure of his touch and exposing a gleaming channel of rubbery puffiness glossed by dark oils of red. She felt the warmth of his quivering tongue as he brought it down to her thigh's bloodied insult and skirted his mouth's sprawling muscle up and down the stretch of the lesion in frenzied worship.

Although she had anticipated tenderness and sensitivity she had imagined traditional for approaching virgins, all expectations were dashed as she sensed his groin slam against her, disciplining the newly fluted sex organ puckering along her thigh as best he could while it flourished with blots of blood. She scarcely had the opportunity to notice the round vent in the mattress participating in the activity. It, too, flinched wildly, swallowing whatever fluids it could salvage pooling about the contours of its wrinkling lips.

"W-w-wait–! Wait–!" she stammered, sobbing.

She jerked as she felt Francis grip himself and work his purpling crown of stiffness deeper inside. Red flowers of tepid stickiness lapped up with every thrust. She felt his glans press against the greasy knob of her femur jutting out from the meaty brawn of inflated tissue as though it were the clitoris of the makeshift female sex he had created. Zelda hoped her stirring in exhausted agony like an uncomfortable animal would interrupt his ardency in deepening the gash; however, it did the opposite, as her soft tortured gasps seemed to stimulate him as his pelvis wildly thrust against her wound with wet slapping sounds.

Zelda sensed the mouth of her thigh's lesion pout at Francis's absence as he drew himself out with a groan of fulfillment. In the momentary intermission, she couldn't help but bring her quivering hands down to the wound, touring her fingers about the contours of its sulking mouth. She winced in agony at the persistence of her fingers that searched as if urgent to find some sort of token or sign of womanhood. In her innocence, she had not known what it would look like or feel like; all she learned now from the betrayal of her bruised sex was that what she had been searching for was absent and could most likely never be there.

Zelda had little time to grieve as Francis collapsed by her side, the softness in his dwindling erection still pressed against her and damp with her blood as she felt it wilt on its side like a plump slug. It was the round opening in the bedding that had been ideal in its patience until now to swallow her gender whole that proposed a new threat to Zelda as it gargled what leaked from the yawning valve in her thigh. Now, four times longer in length and eight times broader in width, Zelda saw the fully distended orifice chortled as it sang through wreaths of their juices, yet still visibly tempering its enthusiasm as though it were anticipating far profounder rewards yet to come.

As though expecting, Francis slipped off the mattress and rolled his body onto the floor, out of the way. Although Zelda was visibly perplexed by Francis's sudden retreat from the sanctity of their altar, her puzzlement did not last long as more of the bedding ripped, seams splitting and the sound of steel coils arguing vehemently as they chafed one another to accommodate some sweltering force burgeoning beneath the cushioning. As the face of the mattress fanned open, filleted like the underside of a horseshoe crab, Zelda's thigh was inhaled by the crevice already jellied with a generous tarn of her blood.

Her entire body palpitated as the flayed nerve endings in her open wound were exaggeratedly sensitive to the prick of the round steel coils that had begun to soften as though they were membranous tendons that coiled about her legs with an uncompromising grip. She made soft, confused cries while more than half of her lower body was dragged under and outstretched her arms while pleading to Francis, who sat against the wall with his eyes closed.

Zelda cried one final time, the resolve in her organs and bones loosening to nonbeing as she sensed more of the glandular springs braid themselves about her body and yank her down below the bloodied cushioning. Her shoulders, neck, and head were swallowed whole. Ripples of blood and seminal fluid murmured up in quiet bubbles, detailing where she had once been but was unquestionably no more.

Once its voracious appetite had been satiated, the lips of the bed's vaginal imitation puckered. Francis watched as the contours of its shape flex, gargling licks of what it must have considered soggy goodness. Satisfied, the ribbon of gaping muscle fixed in the cushion of the mattress that ran from the crown to the bottom began to shrink, narrowing its prodigious width and shriveling like a fatigued male sex organ as it dwindled to the mere unassuming vent it had been before. The outlet wheezed, stammering the occasional hiccup of blood and semen.

"There," Francis shouted disgustedly at the small dimple in the bedding. "That's what you wanted, isn't it?"

Not unlike his other sessions of momentary genital easement, he shrank with repulsion as he crossed to the nightstand, his feet careful to avoid random slicks of fluid, and re-lit a half-finished cigarette. He did not grieve, but rather panted with relief at a task that was clearly unavoidable. His easement was fleeting, however, as all respite was ruined at the sound of fluids seething beneath the mattress, foamy giggles of wetness detailing an ache that suggested an appetite for more. He noticed the imprint of a hand expanding from beneath the mattress, ballooning the pillows of cushioning and inflating them with threads of palpitating capillaries.

"What are—?" he murmured, unable to finish the question.

The vent answered Francis almost instantly as it sputtered a cough, its width violently jerking open with a gag of regurgitated steam. Without warning, the breach in the bedding furiously expelled a generous clot of what appeared to Francis as a mucous-like gel that splattered the ceiling with a vulgar thud.

Another fountain of mucous followed, this one flecking the wall's paneling with syrupy globs, dribbling down the molding in glistening streams. More releases were made, all varying in their trajectory as if the faucet in the mattress was proficient enough in its otherwise undeveloped nature to skillfully direct its aim, administering each spew of gelatinous discharge with a distinct purpose.

Francis recognized there was nothing benign about the vent's dismissal of ejaculate or regurgitated gaps of air as each cough of solutions was more violent than the last. While the glutinous-like fluid drooled down the paneling, hardening to gossamer blankets of fidgeting tissue, the bedding's venereal duct spouted a collection of veiny threads glossed with translucent oils. The flaccid ends of the filaments hooked into the floorboards with what appeared to be curled metallic phalluses distending from the pinkness of their rounded glans.

"You were supposed to–" Francis stammered, horrified.

Zelda's eyeball wrinkled open from a fatty sheath of gleaming tissue varnishing the wall. Her other eyeball pleated the pillows of sodden fat on the opposite wall while Francis saw a pair of lips furrow, puckering, from the globs of ejaculate drooling from the ceiling.

"Beautiful woman." The lips on the ceiling moved with the sound of Zelda's voice but were distinctly absent of the nervousness of her usual stammer.

Francis gripped the shears he had dropped on the floor and wielded them as though they were a token redeemable for salvation from the monstrous. It was then that he heard tortured shrieks of anguish, not entirely dissimilar from the vicious howling of newborns. The cries billowed up and out from the vent in the bedding, their exasperation echoing in what sounded to Francis as a cavernous pit of unending carrion.

"What – w-what is that–?" Francis screamed.

"Yours and mine," Zelda's disembodied voice replied. "Another rite of passage for womanhood. Birth."

Francis staggered back, slipping on the tarn of mucous pooling on the floor, as the first of what sounded to be a gathering of new visitors crowned at the vent of the bedding, heaving its body up onto the mattress by grabbing hold of the firming cords of tissue and dragging along with it a thick clot of placenta. Although far more accomplished in the use of its bodily functions than most newborns, its anatomy was considerably underdeveloped with its bulbous head too great for the smallness of its blackened carapace.

It heaved itself forward by its arms while its palsied legs thrashed like rubbery tentacles. The creature brought its proboscis up and its lips wrinkled with contentment as, in its immaturity, it clearly knew no shame for its repugnant appearance. Its face, however, was the most remarkable aspect of all as, despite its caking of ash and blood, confessed a birthmark just like his father's.

Francis screamed at the recognition and lurched away, his arms flailing. He took no more than two steps before he slipped on the gel thickening on the floor. Although desperate to right himself, the strain of Zelda's fluids cemented against him like glue and weighed his whole body down. He fought with an effort that was no match for the strings of jellied slime pulling against his arms and legs and discouraging any further movement.

His fingers reached for the door only to find it was now nothing more than a membranous panel sheathed by cushions of greasy muscle so pale that they appeared translucent while beading laurels of Zelda's bodily fluids. As Francis lurched forward, his face pressing against the tissue of paneling rippling with the clot of membranes and nerve endings, he watched her tongue crease the tissue and sprawl out in an exaggerated curl.

He shuddered while her tongue violently flexed against his cheek as if in an urgency to convince that she would care for him just as he had so often taken care of her.

"I'll tell you when to move," she whispered to him.

Sheldon Woodbury

A Dream Come True

A booming clarion call erupted in the crackling fires of Hell and the monstrous army took flight like a thundering maelstrom of howling black bats. Massive wings flapped through the choking ash and searing haze until they shattered through the soot covered rock above. Red eyes blazed with an inferno like glow as they ascended through the endless layers of sulfurous rock. The underworld horde broke through the last barrier with a volcanic roar and their startling appearance threw a withering shadow over the world below. It was a sight never witnessed before, but a new age was coming, the end of times, when everything was going to be dead and dark.

The Devil was in the lead of course, a frightening colossus that seemed even more gruesome in the early morning light. It was the daemon king, the avatar of evil, a blasphemous creature finally free from its smoldering prison of fire and gloom. The gargantuan shadow from its twisted horns, cloven hooves, and fire-crusted wings grew larger and larger the higher it soared. Its cackle was blaring and triumphant as it glowered at the non-believers below. They were seeing what they thought was just a religious myth suddenly flapping in the blue sky above.

It unleashed a comet like fireball and the horrified humanity scattered like ants. Millions fried in the blink of an eye, which it took as just the first of countless more pleasures to come. The noxious stench of burnt flesh and swirling smoke erupted up like a billowing fog, filling the sky with a churning blackness. It unleashed another and the rippling ocean instantly came to a steamy boil, bringing more charred death bubbling to the surface.

Charging higher and higher, it embraced its freedom as a delirious miracle that was long overdue. After an eternity trapped in the infernal sewers of Hell, a realization had suddenly appeared deep within its cavernous consciousness. It knew with an absolute certainty that the time had come to escape. It didn't question its origin because the impossible happened in Hell all the time, but more agony and despair had always been the result.

Until now.

The struggle between Heaven and Hell had been an ongoing battle since the dawn of time, with victories and losses on both sides. It was the secret history of good and evil waged in the shadows by inscrutable forces never fully revealed to the world of man, but the bowels of Hell were now overflowing with damned souls, so maybe this is where its newfound power had come from, the sheer mass of evil now writhing in its fires.

One of the cruelest perversities was that time itself was even more brutal. Every second seemed like a never-ending eternity, so eternity itself was an infinite horror multiplied even more. The surreal inflictions of pain and punishment were so far beyond the scope of endurance, each second in Hell was an abomination without boundary or limit.

That's why its rage at the God who had put it there was unbounded too. Even now, rising higher and higher in the churning black sky, its anger, and ferocity roared like a living thing, consumed with a ravenous hunger for revenge that propelled it at an even more charging pace, its monstrous army flapping below like a howling black cape.

Hell had its own rewards too, and these it would share with the God it despised with every charred chunk of its hideousness. After endless eons inflicting unbearable torture and pain, it was a soulless connoisseur with a devious insight into the intricacies of both. Its underworld power was beyond any threshold or boundary the mind could imagine, even that of the most wretched and insane. This power it would share in all its abominable forms with the God it hated, and its clinging legion of angels too.

A rumbling chuckle rattled deep inside as it imagined the battle to come between its howling horde and the coddled white angels made puny and weak by their whimpering sanctity. While its torturous skills were more myriad and precise, its underworld army was adept at torture and misery too. Each damned soul, forged in Hell, to become the daemonic extreme of its unholy sin. They were daemon molesters, daemon slaughterers, and daemon sadists, all reconfigured into a wicked new form by the transforming fires of Hell.

If it were a different kind of creature, it would almost feel pity for the desecration to come. Heaven was going to be a killing field of mutilated angels wailing over the death of their God.

After the strangling darkness of its entombment below, the new sights and sounds should have held more allure, but it was too eager for the apocalyptic battle to begin. It also knew that all of creation was a strange kind of mysterious mirage, including the hallowed heights of Heaven and the fiery black depths of Hell. It was all part of a cosmic mystery. How it knew this didn't matter, because that was part of the puzzle too. It didn't diminish its raging fury or burning hunger for revenge, it just stopped it from caring about the unknowable line between what was real and what was not.

Its journey to Heaven was a dreamlike assault that could have an eternity or just seconds, it had no way of knowing; it seemed to be through an abandoned wasteland of ghostly galaxies, skeletal nebulas, and dying universes, because all that seemed to be part of it. However, the opposite was also true, and the vastness of space suddenly looked like God sculpted it into a phantasmagoria of divine perfection.

None of it mattered because it wasn't interested in puzzles or mysteries, only the profound and final destruction of God.

Then, without any warning at all, there it was in all its sickening glory, the towering gates of Heaven glowing in the celestial blackness ahead. It was not disappointed or surprised at all, because the vision was exactly what was expected, a majestic white barrier with two radiant angels standing as guards.

It paused for just a quick moment to savor the terrified look that instantly filled the angel's eyes. Then it gave the clarion call to attack. Its horde of fire-crusted daemons let out a blaring howl that shivered the towering gates below, then swooped down with an astonishing speed and barreled through the glowing white gates with an even more monstrous howl.

What was so stunning was how the massacre that followed was like a healing salve to all the anger and fury that had accumulated during its time in Hell. Here too, time was different in much the same way. Every second was meant to be a glorious eternity to bask in the holy bounty of God. Now those eternal seconds were filled with the exact opposite, the scorching power and fury of Hell.

The daemon army attacked without mercy or restraint, savaging Heaven with inferno red eyes. Their wicked assaults came from every direction as the terrified angels scrambled to hide. The daemons were too brutal and fast, so the hurricane swirl from their flapping wings quickly filled with severed angel parts.

It marched through all this, as Heaven became the splattered killing field it had lusted for. It didn't bother to step around the mangled angels, but kicked them aside like unwanted trash. These were the lucky ones; others lay bound on top of makeshift altars, and forced to endure atrocities that could only have originated in Hell. The daemon molesters and daemon sadists were performing their own rituals on the whimpering angels begging for a mercy that would never come.

Another dark chuckle rattled inside.

Welcome to my world.

It continued its triumphant march though the death and despair as its giant black wings fluttered behind it. Where there was once beauty, light, and holiness, now there was none. That left just one last fight and then it would all be done.

It saw a shimmering light ahead so it quickened its pace. It marched over the mutilated angels and past the makeshift altars of torture and abuse. Now all of Heaven looked like Hell and that was a pleasure it embraced with something close to joy. Now the glow was so bright it could barely see through its blinding light.

The sight it finally came upon was not a complete surprise, but stirring nonetheless. It was a colossal figure lying on a celestial bed of clouds. It was robed, and bearded, its radiant face only partially seen. The sight immediately brought back its burning rage with an even more hellish ferocity. It had no qualms about killing God while it slept, so it marched to its side with fiery steps..

That's when the real horror washed over, a cosmic pain it had never felt before. It knew all of creation was some kind of mysterious mirage, and now it knew why. The mirage was a dream, and the dream was a nightmare, and it was somewhere inside this sleeping God. That meant all the atrocities behind it, the death and destruction in Heaven and all the horrors in Hell, were just that, God's nightmare.

Then it knew this with even more certainty as it felt an urge to share its depravity with the sleeping colossus in front of it. It slowly reached out with its fire-crusted claws and gently pulled open the glowing white robe. Another dark chuckle rumbled deep inside, because this could still be a dream come true.

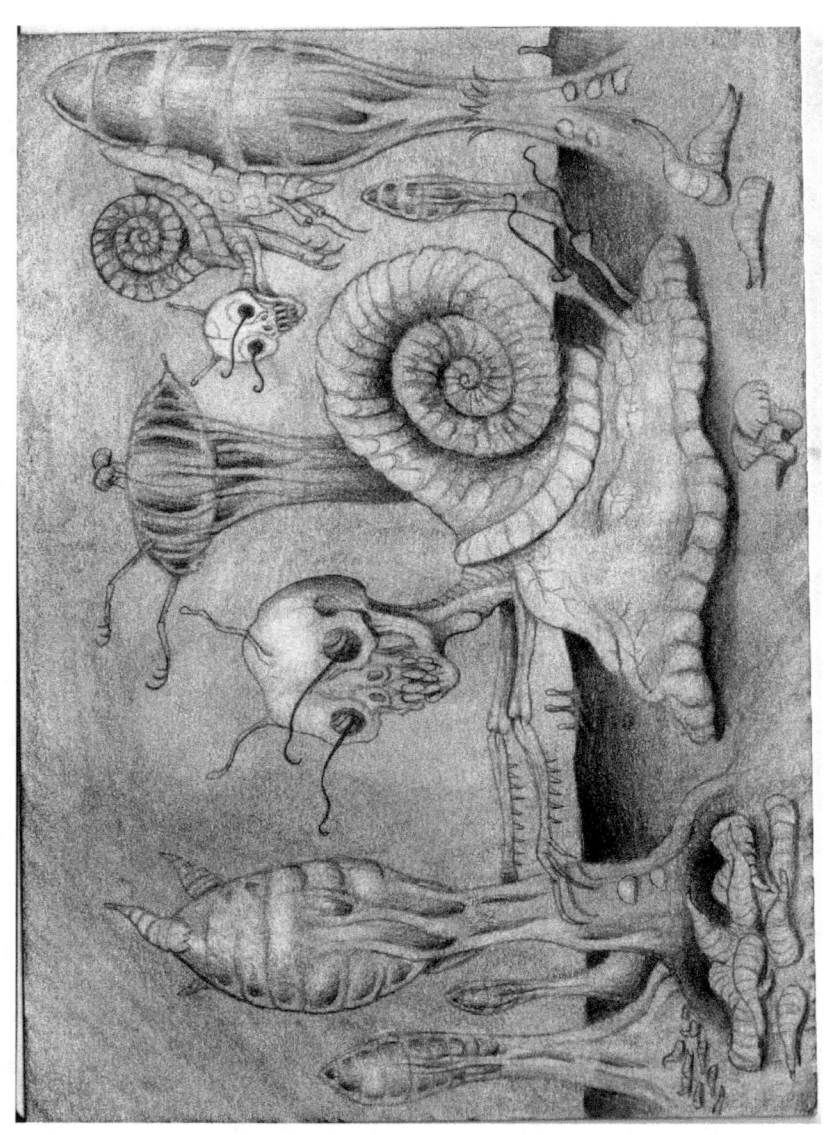

Trevor Hallam

Glass of Corrupted Brilliance

My birth into this ghastly world was unwanted. A pillage made by thieves of purity, their blood coursing with hot, synthetic adrenaline, hearts speeding with tainted spoils charged to them for the price of false antiquities, pumping its disease to their once promising minds, corroding their thoughts and manipulating their actions, which God gifted to all men and named Free Will. Brains exploding and birthing desperation, they purged discretion and defiled the sanctity of an innocent's virtue. Infected blood rushed from heart to mind to loins, and so the monster spewed from them to her, a vile concoction.

I was born from the wretched last dream of a dying woman. My first breath sputtered against the bosom of comfort, in violated arms. A burden to her good name and a blemish on God's Good Grace, I was cast away. Lived my youth in a convent of lies and secrecy, the abuse for heresy punishable by the lash of cold leather that burned the flesh it cleansed. My inquisitiveness was considered contemptible, blasphemy. Fear dwelled and brought weakness to my heart. I lived with the hate of fear, and I promised to adapt, conform, and conquer, but it was no good. The punishments became more severe, until I no longer feared such hate, the hate of my fear. The hate of fearful men.

Belief soured, poisoned by the laws and judgments of these fools in robes who worshipped Power, fed on the flesh, and drank of the blood. My soul to Hell, I did not care. The lusts and perversions I witnessed caused peril. This prison was my hell, but a place I could one day escape. I lived as their ward, listened to scripture and the rules of the realm. I lived as instructed, secretly striving to be better than them, rapists and pillagers in their own holy way, and knew my sweet freedom would come, sooner than the God of their faith. I would laugh and cry when my day arrived. No more blunt trauma or suffering caused by their distaste of me, simply for wanting to be better than my fathers.

So came the day, as I foretold it. It was the time of longing, that wondrous period when I came of age and escaped their tyranny, finally free to write about dreams in which they were dead, and to educate myself as I deemed fit. It was in my studies, in halls of historical relevance, that I met the girl whom I loved first, the heroine in my most passionate tale, the Queen of my Empire, and I was a humble servant of her Order. To win her was beyond my reach, though to adore her was easy. I was shameless in my attempts to sway and impress, all due to that view her elegance offered. To speak to her was a triumph all its own, and to hear her gentle voice was a blessing, more spiritual and more brilliant than any depiction of Paradise. Her heart was large and inviting, but for the time, sealed shut and promised to another, whose intentions were unlike my own—devious and badly tempered, willing to cause harm at a callous breath or a contemptuous glance. Still, she lingered in the forefront of my busy mind, her zeal, and wit consuming my every thought. All of my plans became secondary to her happiness. I prayed to gods I could never believe in, whose wisdom and regulations resembled too closely the deceit and the lies of manipulators long dead, echoing their fears for things confusing and different, which they could not understand or embrace. I was willing, more than ever before, to live by their clout of hypocrisy so I could show her the scars of countless indignities administered by allies of intricacy.

Her disregard always greeted my endeavors and I thought she must be a creation of the devil. Could it be that she was a prisoner to the hateful swine who shunned her ideas and laughed to spite? Perhaps, that hateful lover's demise would free her, as I thought I was freed, only to burden myself in the chamber of her needs. I'd be her rescuer and tear down the walls of mortification.

I spied their fevered dance one warm afternoon, the flames of jealousy tingling my nerves. Following him away, I struck him down with tremendous blows. His life poured out and coated the edges of the cold stone, and I opened his canvas to remove the source of his being. It throbbed once in my hand, throbbed no more. I sank my teeth deep and consumed the final remnants of energy, his body, and soul.

The girl grieved, and I did blame her. I begged her to shed not one more tear, but realized a startling knowledge that made me sizzle. Face clouded and creased in remorse for he who had gone, she spoke the sentence I dreaded to hear.

"Do I know you?" she asked.

"Don't you know the one who loves you?" I said to her.

She wished for the lover I had sent off in disrepair. Her glorious eyes shattered like priceless glass and washed over me like acid. In the drained sockets, former windows to her soul, I saw seething hate, empty and black.

Perhaps shame kept me alive. I should not have existed at all, but some dark blessing made it so. Now, what to do with this life? It seemed only natural that a beast spawned through tragedy and bad taste should become the monster I knew destiny demanded me to be. I would save her, that emerald of mine, and strip away the aggression—it turned her ugly. No grievances or spite, I had hope she would be welcomed wherever the tarnished blade sent her.

When I felt the sadness go, I rested in a pool and gave aim to the future. Where did one go when his first love had gone, part of him forever, but only within? I still feel her in my heart, her essence pumping through these muddied veins, cleansing them with her love. She was an offering, thanks for the existence obtained.

It said that God loves his little torments, and will visit such consignment on his unsuspecting flock without warning. For years, I believed in goodness but now I thrived with the bad. Fantasies of destruction, hysteria, and blooming death like a black-petal rose, thorns dripping red, consumed me. The human race is wanderers and conquistadors. I despise humanity—yes, the very fabric of that which I am. One discovery does not quench the thirst. One state and one province, one nation, one world, never enough. Happiness—true happiness—comes with a price. It comes from experience and self-indulgence. Money affords happiness. This is truth.

Love ... Love? Love is for the poor, the wretched, and the discarded.

On I go, my dreams and talents in hand, into manhood. I quelled the hunger with what I could spend.

Despair set in once again, nuzzled my heart, and thoughts of death consumed. God was playing, finding joy in my humility. He delivered the Woman—how does the cliché go? The love of my life. She came to me, a beautiful thing, with power that energized my soul and brought gladness to my life, not yet bought and paid in full. I was ready to live and die by her command. Wonders and sights, ideas and laughter, she offered to me. She banished depression and annihilated all those things I'd become. But as quickly as she'd come into my life, she was gone, taken. A man of spite, much like the man I had been, stole her away. The repeat of history left me the fool, disturbed what remained of my humanity. One day, I would find her, and with her the captor, who could have been me were it not for her. I would kiss her that day, love her once permitted, and kill the bastard thief in my ecstasy.

I am corroding. I am no one. I am nowhere. Nothing.

The burden was mine. Without her, I was empty, alone. Men made threats for me to be gone and women ran screaming while their children laughed and called, shouting disdain, calling me the dead man who walked in defiance of the laws of life and the After. In the ground or on a flaming pyre, I should be, and right they were, I thought. Death, itself, had seized my soul and left behind a shell. Had I been aware, as I am now, I'd have chased them and fed on their skin, raped their mothers and slaughtered the men. Instead, I wandered on, saving my vengeance. How glorious to have her again, to soothe and set at ease the frustration and sorrow brought by the loss endured.

In my search for her, I met others who did not fret or turn tail and hide, whose own misfortunes and agonies outweighed that of my own, leaving them careless of the danger others thought lurked. I fed upon their sorrows, greedily, sating the hunger I had repressed.

There was a child, mere days shy of the trials of adolescence, in a rundown shelter, and she looked at me, unafraid, too much in misery and much too deprived of a life she deserved. She asked for my help, skin on bones and in need. Looking into her eyes, blurred and glossy, age of a crone behind those windows, I explained there was nothing I could give to make it better.

"I cannot save myself, let alone others, especially a child already reduced to such tatters."

I left her in that dankest place, her grief out of mind.

A man in rags, filthy and diseased, was next to disrupt my way, and I with no penance to offer. He growled and accused, this rabid thing, so I pushed him away. A dagger reflected a blinding glint, and I managed to avoid the kiss of its careless wrath. I ran, not to be humble, and left the man in his rag tuxedo to his madness, happy not to have succumbed to his rage. I thought to return with an instrument of my own, and carve into his flesh a warning, to keep away and not underestimate the sickness in me but as it was, there were more pressing issues on which to attend.

My travels continued with no end in sight, and I met one other before I could rest. She came to me from shadows, a ghostly sight. A slave to the dusk, she was broken and used up. Foulness aside, she said what was right, and we fell into talking. I told of my search and she laughed, practicing the art of audacity, offering her tainted pleasures for a gentle fee, promising amnesia if, for an hour, I let her have me. Thoughts of her illnesses, mean and contagious, sickened my senses. Her rotted womb, so abused, filled with the contaminants of a thousand sickly degenerates before me, was no longer capable of producing life, only able to birth perversion. Still, the heat rose, festered and stewed, and became appetizing; to enter her cozy just for this eve, feel the incessant burn and the emptiness inside. I let her corrupt me, not for love, only hate and lust. Her, she cared not. I was not her charmer, just a customer, one of many.

As I swam in her sea, feeling the fire, drowning in delight, I gazed into eyes familiar to me. Her body and mind had captured the spirit, so tired and used long before when she was but a skinny whelp pleading for help, refused by me. I'd carried on my way. Had it truly been so many years? So must it be why I am so weary, no longer the man of my youth, but a tired disgrace. I went away from her slumber, her pit of despair. And off she had gone, offering a wink and a quip of familiarity, saying, "Thanks for your help, sir. I knew you'd come through."

And when we parted, I lowered my head to hide my smile.

The locomotives were chugging along at frantic pace, delivering products to outlets, needy consumers desperate for the charge. I watched in purest happiness, the derailment, and loss of screaming cargo, the cacophony of destruction warm against my face, brilliance in my ears. This was godliness, I thought.

This was happenstance. The girl of undaunted faith crossed my path unannounced, appearing like some specter of heavenly knowledge, her belief in the Power unquestioned and something to be admired. Flesh bared and opened to Death, she stood beneath the blazing heat of Heaven's glare, smiling as the cars tumbled and careened by, the screech and grind of dried gears and the clank and smash of steel buckles as they rolled over oiled tracks of melted rails musical bliss. She saw in me the joy and scolded me gently.

"Live through the pain," she instructed. "God will decide when it's time to go."

Questions arose as to what made her strong and, without shame, she said, "Jesus raped me and placed the faith inside, and now I can go happily into the embrace of the Saints."

She raised her arms, slit wide to gush, wetness flowing down in eager rivulets, following the curves of delectability and dripping to puddles at her dirty feet. With her face turned up, I saw the promise in her smile.

"I am ready, now, my loving Lord, who desecrated my beauty and harmony for unselfish pride, so as to save me from the torments of wicked mortal men. Take me, if it please."

For many hours, I watched, waiting for her to ascend. I grew tired of the farce and left her to her saintly pose. Days later, I returned to the spot with thoughts of her smile. She remained, arms limp and sagging, face somnolent and confounded and turned to the sky, forever waiting for her darling defiler to complete the scandal.

And the girl was no longer certain of misled convictions as I watched her age and wilt, a reminder of life's many disappointments. The tears strolled down dusty cheeks, black, and she cried out, a pitch of despair and mingling anger that unnerved. I trembled at her loss. To this day, she stands under duress, face worn beyond her years, and she always cries and has forgotten how to pray. I hope mercy will shed its light, and the old crone will be rewarded for her naivety.

All who live and all who strive lack in virtue and serve themselves. I am no different. These fools, so petty, squander, and abuse what is theirs, hoping the next domain is kinder. After a time, so wasted with neglect, the inevitable happens. The ignominious ending that begets happiness, but offers none. And so it seems I've become one of the self-absorbed, nothing to live for.

I want her to destroy all I ever wanted, so that there is only her.

There she stood, enigmatic, and for long breaths I could not move, nor could I call out her name, but only stand still and shudder. She lavished in the embrace of her captor. Polluted rivers flowed down the crumbling slopes of this tired landscape, where sacrilege had muddied its hills, froze the vegetation, and brutalized the view. Rabid dogs of fire and ash rose from the devastation, howling, and attacked, downing their prey. They fought over the feast, biting and tearing the flesh until, finally, my rival was no more than a few scraps of tissue and a hunk of bone, to which my lady wailed and shed rivers of her own. Turning on me, she caused my hounds to retreat, tails curled snugly between their legs, their whines and yelps a vibrant reminder that she would not be frightened by a pack of old mutts.

Shouting in fierce sorrow, she said to me, "I hate you, dog, for this which you've done!"

Weak and de-clawed, I whimpered, "It was you who brought this anguish. I loved you, dearly."

"Your love is false and untrue. It's the idea of belonging to something that interests you. You are a coward."

And so saying, she turned from me, kneeling to the scraps of her dispatched lover, whom she, herself, had maimed by that awfulness called Betrayal.

My anger took toll, but I was too neutered to act, so I spewed derivatives of my ignominy.

"I want to peel off your false face, this curtain of lies, and stick it to a wall of hate, bullet-ridden from countless executions. Though it trembles, ready for collapse, the apathy holds it together. I'll let your hidden features of innocence rot, to show the sheen of your black skull, lined with imperfections, your true identity beneath the mask."

And to that God I hate, I said, "I want to burn out your fraud, your fascist deceit and useless promises of better things. I'll feed to you the consumerism you've forced on me with the inadequate products of a billion dreams, and crack your bones while you feed, regurgitate, feed. Swallow and choke. And I'll chew out my own bitter tongue and place it in the stew along with the others, my penance, my confession, the mind guilty."

My errors mirror the errors of all, and I admit to my ignorance and worthlessness, and admit hypocrisy. Knowing thyself, it is easy to loathe and be subject to the loathing of others all. My love for one is immense, undying, with no doubt. My pithy actions warrant excuse, but none I have.

Mourning pieces of her loss, she picked up his lips—not much more remained—and kissed them in her palms. Severed and ripe, she tucked them away for safekeeping and turned to scowl up at me from her place near the ground.

I cannot remember a time I felt more shame. I did not love her, as she deduced, but thought I could. I've brought only anger and pain. I need do nothing else.

Now I am a man with a debt still unpaid, who sips from the soup of defeat, losing himself inside the deepest bowl. This is simply a pain that will not do. Every man needs a purpose. I have found mine.

I dreamt a place hidden by death, an institution of the Impure, where the land is barren and heat beguiles rage. The fires scorch, blackened landscapes split. Constructions grow only to crumble and fall, and rise up again creations of life—House of Greed. And the sky, slate-gray and pitch, rains down fumes to keep the rage ablaze. Pain and misery begets the anguishing, but all I feel is indifference. The heart opens, spillage spoils the trenches and pits, dank oceans, acidic lakes, molded riverbanks. Sorrow drowning hopes and fires lapping lust.

I look about, eyes numb and dry. Eliminate the hellishness, stamp out the flames, clear the skies of plague and give the hopeless the lies they crave and recognition will peak. I know this place, this life after. It is the world, the forgotten Empire. This revelation clear, I glance to the sour clouds, the illusion lost. I feel nothing. Rot and remorse corroded away, I see all. I see everything.

And perched high on a tower of deception, observing the familiar bore and shamed by thoughts of regression, an Angel sighed.

And so it was that I set out to pay my debt.

"So here we are, new friend called Angel. I've spoken my tale against better judgment, and now there is but one thing left. My destiny, of course, my purpose is not to love or change the world. It is simple enough, when in the company of such an illustrious guest as you. All I want is to see it all come down, the false brilliance shattered."

The Angel, breath like splintered shards against my face, said, "These things are glories compared to the misfortune that waits. Allow me the honor to show what I mean. I shall grant the request and the maniacal Lord you shall see."

"Show me," I said, leaning close.

"No more warnings or advisories to come. The next you will know is the place of eternal woe."

I was led into the callous wasteland, miles from the nearest soul, from the most thriving city to the tiniest village, where monsters fed. Wind unearthed them and they crept to follow, never daring to narrow the distance for fear of consequence.

"There will be anguish," said the Angel. "Immense agony."

On our way to that most unholy venue, our paths crossed with faces of the past. My mother stood watching, birthing a snake that slid from within and wrapped about her throat, squeezing and pulsing, until she could take no more. I left her behind, as I, too, had been abandoned. The wind-blown dust swept her up.

I saw lovers on display for my viewing pleasure but cared not. My first love, happy without me, and all around, victims of mine, buried in the ground. They rise to watch me go. I hope they're as unhappy in death as I am in life.

I saw the child, become the diseased whore, and watched as she fed a baby her tit. The creature bears a striking resemblance; but shall I spare shame to such an abject little beast? I moved on, never looked back when I heard the screams of the child-crone and baby battered to death by the man in rags, who gave to them the light of day reflected on the blade.

Into the desert's depths, air still and heavy, humid and almost too much to take, and we came to a place where the sand was heated to glass. The Angel, he crouched and touched the black crystal, told me it was a window, and to peep through would diminish sanity, for this was the Glass of Corrupted Brilliance.

"See, here, what you've invited. Prepare for a world grown from hate and fear, desire and longing," said the Angel. "A final place of being. Eternity."

The Angel's face sprung thorny hairs, and brutal horns, dripping with the hot grief of countless sins, poked from his tempered brow. Tarred feathers sprouted from his back, spanning triumphantly to cast a vile shadow. The floor of obsidian splintered beneath our feet. Eyes of pitch ensconced existence, and I drowned in their depths. Weightless, I plummeted, shards showering like a vicious torrential downpour. The darkness consumed, making the descent a near-thoughtless excursion. There was a dream of two lovers embraced, melting in ecstasy, becoming one. And they were happy, truly.

The failure I've accepted defeats the urge once held for success and is now my closest friend, one that holds me close to its mighty breast, reassuring the doubts and fears with a grace so loving it borders on perverse. But what are friends for, if not to drag us down from the highest cloud and remind us of who and what we really are under the muck?

And who am I? My friend assures me I am the fake, the false creator of my own dying universe. My friend tells me with morbid glee.

Who am I? An escapee. A derelict. A forgotten opportunity, on stowaway. An insight. An imagination. A thought, little more.

Here is where I belong, denied of simple pleasures, the many broad things out of reach, out of my control. I could learn to accept that, and move on as I have lied about before.

It is all I have left.

Essel Pratt

The Beast Beckons

When I was a child, I had cancer.

Youth prevented me from realizing the grave danger my body endured. I felt weak, tired, and unable to focus on the simplest tasks, so I slept. At times, I would not wake for a couple of days as my body was fed intravenously, drawing essential nutrition from a bag that dangled precariously overhead as sterile machinery beeped around me. I had no idea how close to death I was, how serious the cancer was; I was just a boy.

Bouts of sleep encaged me within a world of dreams, encompassing me in surreal manifestations of my diseased mind. I've learned that the dreams were natural side effects of my treatments, combined with the terminal cancer invading my body. I didn't know what any of that meant at the time, maybe that is how I unexpectedly beat the disease and found myself in full remission after constant agony of the unforgiving treatments. It was the life I knew, I had no clue existence was supposed to be any different.

One dream invited me into its realm every night, beginning where the previous' left off. Doctors told me it wasn't real, but it was my reality. While awake, I felt comatose; unable to function other than to convey my thoughts via vague facial expressions and vocal grunts. In my dream, I was alive, mobile, and able to feel the life that fought inside of my sickly vessel. It was also a nightmarish land filled with demonic presences hell bent on destroying me inside my slumbering consciousness.

Despite feeling alive inside the dreams, I feared them even more. Lingering in my thoughts, I knew survival depended on waking from the dream. Never knowing which shape my cancerous foe would take, cold sweats drenched me, as my eyes would close. Mechanical beeps would fade from earshot, replaced with demonic moans as the familiar realm faded into view. Sleep was my trial; conviction was death.

Standing on the precipice of a smoldering cliff, red stone crackled underfoot. Each visit, I stood, staring off into the distance, wondering if I would ever reach the flourishing spec of green land that basked in the single beam of sunlight that reached through the turbulent cloudy sky. It beckoned me, although mute, welcoming me into the wash of illumination. I did not know if it offered the gift of life or death, both were desirable rewards for reaching its plateau, in my mind at least.

Only once did I have the opportunity to continue forth toward the Eden; all others pushed me down the opposite path; one of damnation and pain as I battled the demons that attempted to claim my contaminated soul and harvest it for their own nefarious needs. Despite the pain and exhaustion I endured, I fought like a warrior, fine-tuning my skills until the day the forward facing pathway revealed itself for the first time, welcoming me to my final trial.

A rope bridge stretched upon the gap to the other side of the precipice, for the first time I could feel my chest expand as breaths of air filled my lungs within the nightmarish realm. My heart beat echoes within my ears, my skin warm with an insurgent of blood within my veins; for the first time inside the realm I could feel the warmth of my own body instead of being invaded by the chills of Hell's icy flames.

Chemo track marks on my arms stung as kissed by the fangs of a black widow; letting loose the venomous toxins into my cardiovascular system. The agony I endured at the instant of my first breath was unlike anything I had ever felt before, but it let me know I was still alive.

I inhaled the sulfur enriched air, allowing the floating ash to enter my lungs and bring forth further warmth to my core; unwilling to declare defeat before placing my first step onto the bridge; willing to accept all obstacles within my path, despite the end result.

Focused on the Eden ahead, I placed a foot onto the bridge, pressing down upon the greying plank to test for stability. Satisfied it was sturdy enough to hold my frail frame, I ventured forth, one slat at a time, while holding on tightly to the frayed rope rails. My heart thumped harder with each step, anticipating a fall as the boards creaked underfoot and the threads in the rope stretched. Near the middle of the expanse, I felt the bridge droop as the path reached upward from where I stood. Tension on the ropes snapped the individual filaments that made the whole, warning of its collapse.

I accepted my fate, but refused to give in. With one foot ahead of another, I stretched my legs and ran as fast as I could, inhaling the heat in the air as I gasped for breath, determined to reach the other side without falling to my death. With each step, it appeared as though two more foot lengths appeared. I refused to give up until my feet were firmly on the other side, unwilling to damn myself to failure. I ran forth as I pulled myself upon the ropes, closing my eyes to hide the infinite path, not stopping until I lost my footing as I tripped and fell onto the stone surface at the end of the bridge.

Back on my feet, I brushed off the ash that covered the front of my shirt and pants, enduring the burn from its embers. Still looking forward toward Eden, I barely noticed the low rumble of the beast's growl behind me, but the vibrations of its thunderous steps revealed its presence. I turned to face my assailant, ready for its onslaught. However, it stood at the other end of the bridge, staring me down, stomping its feet as though taunting me to come forth to him.

With Eden in reach, I demonstrated defiance and turned away from the beast, proceeding forward to my goal, ignoring the bellowing howl that erupted from the beast's vocal box. In my mind, I knew that the bridge's near collapse under my frail frame could never hold the weight of the massive beast on the other side. The talons on its feet would surely slice the ropes that held it up not. So, I continued forward, paying no attention to its threats.

However, nearly thirty strides in, the roars of the beast seemed to approach, so I turned in time to see the large beast bound across the expanse. It landed with a quake, knocking me to the ground at its feet, within mere inches of being crushed under its weight.

I yelled to the beast, denying it the satisfaction of surrender. A flatulence stench bellowed from its bull-like mouth, causing the few contents of my stomach to flow up my esophagus and vomit onto the ground. Although warm, it sizzled upon the charred ground, smelling worse that the beast's breathe.

I fought to stand, but the beast knocked me back to my knees with each attempt. I felt my body becoming weaker, but refused to capitulate. It was a game for the beast as he flicked me off my feet with a single finger, standing stalwart until I rose again, repeating his assault. Determined to stand my ground, I finally crawled backward away from the beast, my heart pounding inside my chest, feeling like it might explode. My inhalations grew labored, burning with each breath. I felt close to death. I was not afraid, almost happy that a resolution to my pain was near. Yet, my body trembled with intense anxiety that I could not control. Yes, I was scared to death, but not scared of death, if that makes sense.

Underneath me, shards of stone, crystal like in appearance, sliced into my flesh and embedded into my body. Warm blood trickled from their insertion points, reminding me once again that life was still present, although my soul was fading fast. The beast, angry at my retreat, reached out its large hand and grasped me tightly in its palm. I felt my vessel breaking under its pressure until the beast yelped in pain as the shards of crystal bit into its hand. Rather than continue its onslaught, the beast thrust me through the air. My body, feeling weightless, floated with the grace of an eagle, drawing ever closer to Eden.

With the lush green utopia in sight, the excruciating heat of hell gave way to warm breezes and soft winds of springtime. I was on a crash course to my fate, so I let my arms spread wide at my sides, eyes open as large as they could, welcoming my arrival. I don't remember landing, just a bright light then nothingness for a second or eternity. I am unsure which.

I remember waking up after that dream, exhausted weak, my entire body aching. I reached Eden, I know I did, yet I did not feel healed, refreshed, or ready to continue life any further. I just felt like I was existing; nothing more. Yet, although the dream was less scary than any other I had during my cancerous ailment, it was the beginning of a change for my nightmares. For the next few months, the beast became less of a threat and my journey to Eden was less dangerous, until one night the dream started with me standing inside Eden, within a field of flowers, butterflies fluttering about my head. In the distance, I could see a small island, reminiscent of the hell I endured since the cancer invaded my body.

When I awoke from that dream, I felt good, refreshed, pain free. My parents stood at my bedside, smiles on their faces, bursting to tell me that I was in complete remission from the cancer guaranteed to take my life.

In hindsight, the last of the beastly dreams was less scary than the hundreds that preceded it. Yet, I was a only a child, fearing that it would be the end of my life that very night, terrified that I would never see the loving smile of my parents again, never experience the joys of having friends sleep over, find the girl of my dreams, or even have children of my own. I was only a child, but feared missing the stuff a kid my age should not even have been thinking about. Yet, the fear inside me forced me to look beyond my age as I contemplated my eventual demise.

No, the dream of the beast was not very scary, now that I think about it. Yet, it was the one I remembered the most vividly of them all. It hasn't haunted my dreams since then, but I have thought about it from time to time. What makes it more frightening though, after twenty-three years I had the dream once again last night. I was there, in my Garden of Eden, laying in the tall green grasses, listening to the buzz of pollenating bees, and relaxing in the warmth of the sun. That is, until the sky darkened and smoldering heat caught fire to the fauna.

I tried to wake up, but I couldn't. I could only lay there as the world burned around me, helpless as my flesh scorched within the conflagration, hoping the nightmare would end. Just as quick as the apocalyptic chaos arrived, it left, leaving scorched earth in its wake, revealing a large figure standing before me. It took a moment to clear my vision of the blurriness that scarred my eyes. When I did, I realized it was the beast. He did not attack; instead, he pointed toward Hell, with a crooked grin upon his face.

I woke up just after that, leaving the dream world and awaking in reality. I was drenched in a cold sweat, shivering uncontrollably. The pain in my head was intense, still is, familiar as it stabs through my left temple.

Since waking, fright has taken over my every thought. I beat the cancer once, and understood that beating it again would not be possible since they removed a small chunk of my brain in an attempt to rid me of the worst. Any relapse would require more removal of gray matter, leaving me in a vegetative state. I fear the beast in the dream, his beckon to return to hell. I fear my time has come and I am scared to death.

I've experienced friendship, sleepovers, girls, and love. I'm even expecting my first child. Now my fears have changed. As before, I'm not afraid to die. I'm afraid to miss experiences. I may never hold my child, watch it grow, make friends, have sleepovers, discover girls, find love, or meet my grandchildren.

I'm scared to death. All because of a dream.

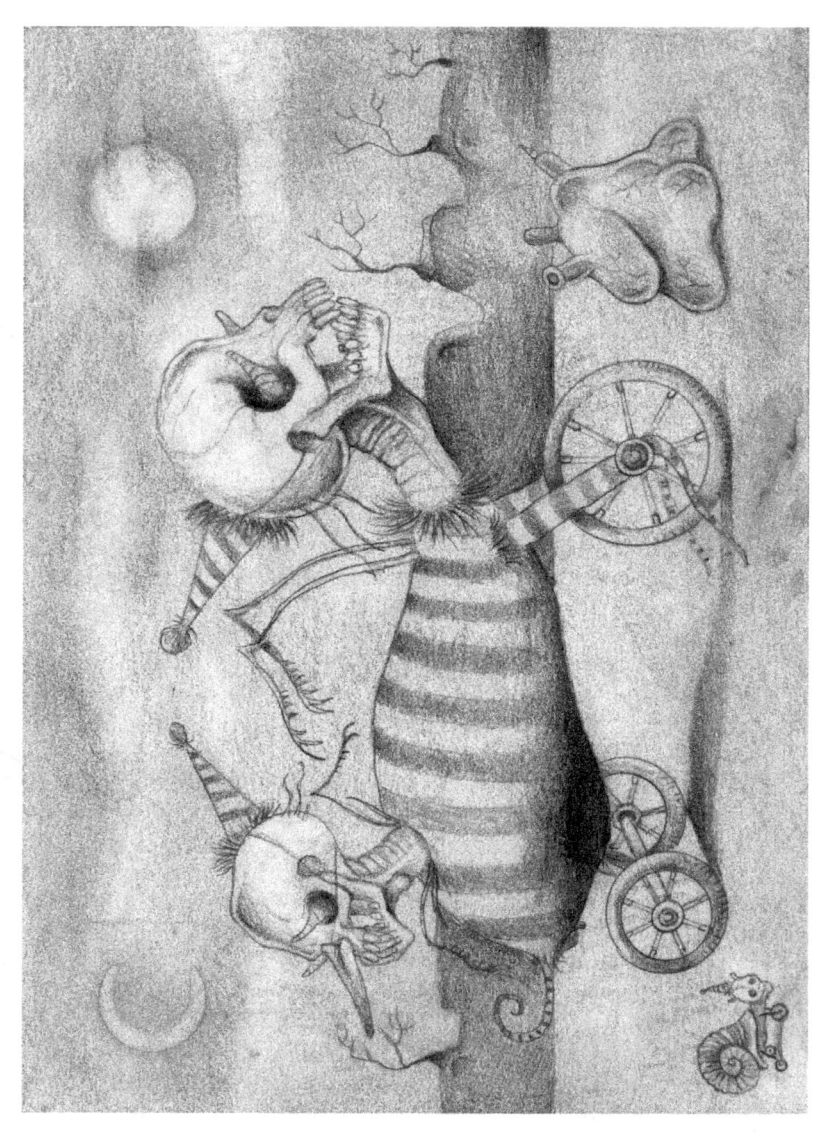

Thomas M. Malafarina

The Gateway

"Explanation separates us from astonishment, which is the only gateway to the incomprehensible." - Eugene Ionesco

"The mind is its own place and in itself, can make a Heaven of Hell, a Hell of Heaven." - John Milton

It appeared to be a gateway of sorts, comprised of an incredible rectangular arch-like framework made from the trunks of enormous trees. There were two vertical columns about six feet around rising perhaps forty feet in the air supporting a massive cross member which spanned the twenty foot wide opening between the two vertical columns. At first, Salazar thought the two verticals had been sunken deep into the earth but he was mistaken. They were actually two huge trees rooted in the ground and only the uppermost branches remained. These branches had grown around and in some places actually fused into the huge cross member holding it securely in place. He had no idea how the massive trunk had gotten forty feet in the air because the thing had to weigh tons.

Salazar wondered what the purpose of this opening had been and more importantly, why he was now standing in front of it. He had no knowledge of how he had gotten to this place. He was a man of countless phobias and being lost in strange and unfamiliar surroundings was just one of them. Fortunately, this was not his worst fear but it was well into the top ten.

He couldn't see beyond the opening as there was a bright luminescent haze blocking his view. He suddenly had a feeling of déjà vu, as if what was happening to him, or at least something similar had happened to him before, yet he couldn't remember a single detail.

Since all around him was nothing but darkness, he felt compelled to step closer and see what lie beyond the opening. One of his other fears was fear of the dark. As a result the blackness, which was on three sides of him had become very upsetting making the luminescent fog, although ominous seem at least slightly more inviting. He took a step forward to look more closely at the huge tree on the right side of the gateway. It wasn't comprised of rough bark as he'd expected but seemed to be made of something of a very smooth texture. Salazar reached out cautiously with his right hand and let his palm gently rest against the strange surface.

An icy chill instantly raced down his spine as he realized what he was touching felt like human flesh, but not warm and living flesh but what he suspected cold and dead flesh might feel like. He had never touched a corpse in his life as he had an aversion to both dead bodies as well as funeral homes in general. Yet he instinctively sensed what he was feeling would be very much akin to dead human flesh.

Again, he experienced a slight familiarity but nothing he could pinpoint. As his fingers rested against the surface, he felt something moving. Looking closer at the fleshy bark, he saw it beginning to pulsate and for the first time he could see something crawling below the undulating skin.

He wanted to pull his hand away in disgust but was transfixed by what he was seeing. On the fleshy surface of the tree above where his hand was positioned, letters began to slowly rise up from the undulating skin. These letters first formed words, which became a cryptic phrase that somehow seemed familiar to him. It read, "As it is, it was and ever will be... again and again for eternity."

What a bizarre message, Salazar thought, in confusion. He realized it was actually a poem of sorts or perhaps just a line from some work he had read once years earlier. Maybe it had been something biblical. He couldn't recall.

After a moment, he noticed an area between his thumb and fore finger where the fleshy surface was beginning to expand outward. A small hole appeared in the skin and the head of a worm-like insect with a tiny, sharp mandible poked out of the opening. Salazar had not only a fear of worms and insects but revulsion for the creatures as well. Before he had a chance to pull away, the thing's horrible pincers grasped onto the flap of skin between his fingers and bit down hard. An unbelievable bolt of pain shot from his hand up his arm and seemed to explode inside his brain.

Salazar finally pulled his hand away in disgust and backed away from the tree shaking his hand wildly trying to get the accursed thing off. He reached over with his left hand and grabbed the creature by its squirming hind end. Knowing somehow that the thing was just second away from burrowing into his flesh, Salazar yanked the thing away from his hand, tearing out a chunk of skin in the process. Then he threw the thing far into the bank of mist and heard the thing screaming as if in agony as it flew.

It instinctively put the wounded area into his mouth expecting to sense the coppery taste of his blood but instead coming away with the tang of something vile, repugnant, and unidentifiable. He spat the putrid substance onto the ground. Although he couldn't see the surface he was standing on because of the penetrating mist swirling about his feet, he would have sworn he heard his own spittle squealing and scurrying away as the insect had done. He worried that the substance might be some sort of poisonous venom that would shut down his ability to breath. Suffocating was probably one of Salazar's greatest fears, next to fear of heights and fear of drowning.

Salazar began to wonder. Was he asleep and having some sort of horrendous nightmare? He didn't believe this to be the case, but then again, who really does know they're dreaming when in fact, they are? The fiery pain he felt in his hand, which was now shooting up his left arm, was certainly real enough. And it didn't seem to be subsiding. If anything, it felt as if it might be getting worse.

In his clouded mind, he was still uncertain whether he should try to pass into the glowing gateway. He was afraid of what might await him in the fog but the blackness surrounding him was unnerving. Then he suddenly heard a deep guttural growling noise coming from behind him. He was unable to see anything, but he could hear deep breathing and the unremitting growling was now getting ever closer. It sounded very big and just as dangerous. He was terrified of wild animals and after what he had just experienced with the strange maggot-like creature he didn't want to confront whatever might be approaching from behind.

Then he heard a rumble and felt the ground beneath his feet began to quake. To his shock, Salazar saw that both trees were somehow impossibly moving closer together pushing up mounds of dirt before them. He looked down and saw the roots had begun to move like dozens of thin creeping legs. He glanced up and saw the massive cross member was coming rapidly downward. If he stayed where he was, he would be crushed.

Seeing no other alternative, he jumped through the gateway and into the mysterious vapor, losing his footing and falling down onto the thankfully soft soil. He rolled, trying to protect his aching left arm. Then he stood up, dusted himself off as best he could then began to walk deeper into the mist. After a few steps, he found himself completely engulfed in the strange fog. He no longer heard the menacing growling behind him. Looking back, he couldn't see the gateway just more of the glowing mist. It was as if passing through the entrance, which he thought had been just a few feet behind him had somehow put him into a place, somewhere perhaps miles from where he had previously been. He understood this instinctively but couldn't comprehend how that could be possible. Again, there was that faint sensation of familiarity.

The first thing he noticed was that his skin immediately began to tingle as the strange haze seemed to cling to his flesh like a glove of moisture. He felt it on his hand, arms, and face. He noticed the fiery feeling had left his hand and arm but a dull pain remained. Then he could feel the strange stinging from the fog on his legs and chest as well. Salazar reached down to touch his shirt and was shocked to discover he was completely naked. He knew he had just been fully clothed a second earlier when he dusted himself off, but now he was as naked as the day he was born. His entire body was tingling, feeling as if the mist was working its way through every pore in his body, crawling deep inside him. He thought about the maggot-creature and shuddered with disgust. Was this strange fog just another form of living thing trying to work its way inside him?

He began to walk slowly and reluctantly forward deeper into the luminescent fog, not because he wanted to do so but because he felt as if he were being drawn inward for some unknown purpose. He looked down and couldn't see his feet, since everything from his chest down was shrouded by the mist.

Salazar suddenly felt a shortness of breath and discovered the air felt thick, hot and heavy, making deep breathing almost impossible. Was this caused by the density of the fog or had that strange mist actually entered his body, surrounded his lungs and begun to suffocate him? He could feel his panic beginning to rise. There was a disgusting stench to the place now, something dank and fishy, perhaps even sulfurous and rotten. His panic piqued as he suddenly realized he could no longer breathe at all. He felt like a drowning man fearful to take a deep breath, knowing his lungs would fill with the vile liquid air.

Finally, realizing his lungs were burning for oxygen he had no alternative. His fear of suffocating was now more real than it had ever been. He opened his mouth, expecting to be smothered by the soupy atmosphere, but to his surprise, he was suddenly able to breathe once again; the air was still vile, hot, stinking, and humid making his breathing labored, but at least he was alive.

After a few dozen arduous steps, he stopped suddenly hearing a series of strange chittering and squealing noises like those made by small animals. A moment later, his blood turned to ice as he felt something brush past his naked ankles. It had only touched him for a millisecond but in that brief moment, Salazar got a very good idea of what the thing might have been. He had felt stiff, fiery hot bristly hairs, which simultaneously felt impossibly slimy with moisture, likely from the fog. He couldn't comprehend how something could feel so hot yet still feel as if it had been coated with thick liquid. His ankles began to burn as his hand had done earlier, then the pain began to climb up his legs. Soon it had spread throughout his entire body and his brain felt as if it were boiling inside his skull. Then just a quickly, the pain subsided and his body was wracked with icy chills.

He wondered what sort of creature was capable of inflicting so much agony so quickly. From that minimal contact, he was able to determine the creature had to be about three feet long and about ten inches tall. An image of a large flaming napalm-covered rat-like creature appeared in his mind and he suddenly trembled from head to toe. Perhaps from fear, perhaps from the icy chill that was finally starting to subside. He heard what sounded like dozens of these creatures and perhaps others more revolting scurrying about the ground all around him. Images appeared in his mind of giant deformed multi-headed lizards, unbelievably long flame-spitting snakes and spiders as large as men with the ability to shoot webbing that not only captured their prey, but which contained an acid-like substance to melt flesh from bone. He had to move on quickly. But just before he did, the words from the poem on the tree came back to him, "As it is, it was and ever will be... again and again for eternity."

He walked on a few steps more wanting to put some distance between he and the strange creatures, not knowing if he was actually leaving one bad situation and walking into another but not seeing how he had any choice. Soon the strange noises died down and he recognized they were far behind him. He suddenly felt a cool, wet crunching sensation under his feet and realized he had left the roadway and had found his way onto some surface that felt like tall cool grass. Up ahead the light seemed brighter and Salazar noticed the mist was blessedly dissipating. Moments later, he found himself standing in a brightly sunlit grassy meadow. Most of the pain and burning had left both his hand and his legs. He looked behind him and could see the bank of fog, which he had just passed through. For the first time since coming into this bizarre place, he felt he might be somewhere at least somewhat normal.

When he turned to look forward once again, he was shocked to see something he hadn't expected to see. Then again, in such an inexplicable world as this one what should he really have expected to see anyway? Standing low in the grass in front of him was a huge land tortoise, more than five feet long and four feet across, of the sort he had seen in wildlife documentaries as a kid. The thing had a massive head that was staring up at Salazar with a look that he could only described as being both curious and surprisingly intelligent. Maybe Salazar was personifying the creature based on cartoons he had seen as a child where aged creatures such as this were often portrayed as having great wisdom.

Feeling not in the least bit foolish - and why should he if he was actually dreaming anyway -Salazar looked down at the creature and asked, "What do you want me to see?" He had no idea where that question had come from or why he thought the tortoise had wanted him to see something. He just had a strange sort of understanding appear in his mind, which told him, that was why the tortoise was there.

The ancient tortoise looked up at him and suddenly inside his mind, Salazar heard an old raspy voice say, "As it is, it was and ever will be... again and again for eternity." Then it slowly pulled its head, legs, and tail into the shell. For a moment, Salazar thought nothing else would happen.

Then impossibly, the top half of the tortoise's massive shell became transparent as if it had been constructed of a glass dome of some sort. Inside Salazar could see perhaps a dozen baby tortoises milling about. These little ones were without benefit of shells, just small pink crawling creatures with tiny tortoise heads and beaks. At first, Salazar thought them quite cute until he looked closer and saw what the creatures were feeding on. There in the center of the transparent shell was a kitten. It was obviously dead, and flyblown with hundreds of maggots crawling about it ripped-open stomach. The tiny tortoises were taking turns tearing off chunks of flesh, fur and innards and devouring them raw. In his mind, Salazar heard high pitch chittering noises similar to what he had heard in the fog. Salazar couldn't remember ever reading about turtles being anything but herbivores and as such was revolted by the sight. Moments later the transparency disappeared and the shell returned to normal, the huge tortoise poked out its head and feet then turned and started to walk slowly away.

In shock, Salazar stumbled backward in the meadow a few steps until suddenly the ground behind him opened up and he fell down into a massive sinkhole. His arms and legs flailed uselessly in the air as he tried desperately to grasp onto something to stop his inevitable fall. He had always feared falling to his death but instead of slamming against solid ground and dying, he landed with a splash in a deep pool of ice-cold water.

As he sank deeper into the water, Salazar struggled to swim upward. He realized not only was he now fully clothed once again, but he was bundled in several layers of shirts, pants and heavy coats, all of which had become sodden with water. The additional weight was pulling him further downward with every passing second. Once more, he could feel his lungs burning with the need to breathe, but unlike the thick atmosphere, this was icy water and he knew if he attempted to breathe, he would most definitely drown.

Just when he knew he wouldn't be able to hold his breath for another second, Salazar landed on the hard floor of the water hole with a thud pushing all of the remaining air from his lungs. To his shock, he looked about him and saw he was no longer underwater but was sitting on the floor of a large room, perhaps thirty feet square. He was once again wearing his original clothing, none of which was wet or even the slightest bit damp. This dream was getting stranger all the time and he wished he could wake himself up.

He looked about the room and saw it didn't so much look like a room, but was a large elevator with two doors, typical of such a device, positioned at what he assumed to be the front of the elevator. However, there were no buttons to select any desired floor, nor were there any lights to identify floor location. He felt a slight motion and the elevator began to move. By the downward pressure he was feeling, Salazar believed he was moving up at an incredible rapid rate.

The elevator seemed to go on forever until finally it stopped. Salazar stood clumsily on wobbly legs. Before the doors opened, a message began to scroll across a light bar, which had just appeared above the door. The message said, "As it is, it was and ever will be... again and again for eternity." It was the same message he had been receiving since coming to this strange place. The doors slowly began to open revealing nothing but complete blackness outside. He knew there was no way he was going to step out into that blackness.

At the same time, the wall behind Salazar began to move forward pushing against his back and forcing him out through the doors into the black void. He had no idea what awaited him out there but his fear of heights and falling into open space was running rampant. The back wall pushed him ever closer to the black void beyond the doorway. Before he realized it, he was standing out in the darkness. To his surprise, he appeared to be on solid ground.

He took about five apprehensive steps forward with his hands extended out in front of him to feel in the blackness for any obstructions. A few steps later, his hand touched something cold and solid cold forcing him to stop. He looked back over his shoulder and saw no sign of the elevator behind him all that surrounded him was more blackness.

Suddenly the area around him was illuminated with blinding white light and Salazar raised his hands to protect his eyes. Slowly he removed his hands and was instantly paralyzed with terror. He found himself standing on a circle of ground no more than one foot in diameter, atop a cropping of stone that had to be several hundred feet above the ground. He didn't want to look down but had no choice. All around him was a vast canyon of immeasurable size with hundreds of similar outcrops far below him. The ground behind him had fallen away leaving him stranded.

But even if he hadn't been too terrified to move, these outcroppings were too far away to do him any good. To make matters worse giant pillars of flames suddenly began to spring up all around him and Salazar could hear the moans and wails of what sounded like a million tortured souls, all writhing in agony somewhere deep within those flames.

Then he understood. This was Hell... his own personal version of Hell. He was about to be forced to join the ranks of the tortured dead. He had thought he led a good life, but apparently he had not. At the instant of this understanding, the pain in his legs returned with a vengeance. The phrase, the poem, suddenly flashed into his mind again, "As it is, it was and ever will be... again and again for eternity." Then he lost his balance, teetered for a moment, then fell down, down into the scorching flames.

He opened his eyes and saw what appeared to be a gateway of sorts, comprised of an incredible rectangular arch-like framework made from the trunks of enormous trees. He had a feeling of déjà vu, as if what was happening to him or something very similar or perhaps a slightly different version of events might have happened to him before, yet he couldn't recall.

Robert Holt
The Wall and Glendalough

Black crayon smudges at knee level marked the names of my earliest victims, and the second grade brutality that I displayed to them: *Bobby Grudding pushed off his bike and skinned his knee, Louis Turtank tripped while going into music class and broke his glasses, and Mary Classier, her hair pulled, messing it up before class pictures*, and so on. I wiped my mouth with the back of my hand. I didn't remember doing that to Mary. I did remember... My eyes scanned up higher on the wall where the names were written in pencil and eventually ink. There it was. *Mary Classier sodomized*. The wall made it sound like some form of rape. It wasn't rape. Seriously, it wasn't rape. It was just...well...

My eyes fell on a single name written in red permanent marker further up the wall. *Bret Dredger killed!* I stepped away from the wall and turned toward the darkness. Panic boiled in my veins. Unable to see my crimes any longer, unable to bare that crime being on my list, I stumbled toward the darkness. "I didn't kill Bret!" My trembling voice was lost in the vacuum that surrounded me. "Are you hearing me?" It was useless; I knew it even then.

I turned back to the wall and saw Bret's shadow on the couch, saw myself sitting on the floor playing Nintendo, saw it through the wall, through the names. What game had I been playing that night? It was one of the war simulations, I think. Romance of the Three Kingdoms 2 probably. Bret and I played that game until we knew it inside and out.

Bret stirred, and I watched myself pick up the vodka bottle and place it in his hands. "I'm done," he said.

I watched myself laugh. "You are done when I tell you you're done. Drink up bitch."

I screamed at the wall as Bret lifted the bottle to his lips and finished it. The dumb fuck finished the bottle. I didn't tell him to do that. I didn't make him bong a pint. *I'm innocent. I'm innocent!* My throat burned as my voice vanished into the darkness behind me. I watched my shadow self stumble to the television and shut it off and then to the couch where Bret was sleeping. I watched as I slapped his face a couple times and laughed. Then I watched as I leaned over him to kiss his lips. Why did I kiss him? That part didn't really happen. I'm not gay. I wouldn't kiss Bret. Had I known he wasn't going to wake up I may have kissed him good-bye; he was my best friend for fuck's sake, but I wouldn't have just kissed him like that. They were making things up now. I screamed at the darkness, "You're making things up now! You bastards!"

When I turned back to the wall, I saw Bret cough and then vomit. Just like that. I walked out of the room, and he died, smothered on his half-digested Taco Bell. I wanted to cry, but instead I hit the wall. I punched it twice and then stopped. There was no pain, but I feared I might break my hand, so instead I put my palms against the wall and lowered my head.

Why were they doing this to me? Why was I the one they wanted? I dropped to my knees. Then a question came to me: Who was doing this? I tried to think backward on the question, but everything leads back to the wall, to the names. I didn't even know where I was or how I got there. I looked up at the wall, and saw Bret's dead eyes staring back at me from the coach. His mouth moved, and I understood he was asking me why.

I stood up. "I didn't do it to you Bret. I wasn't the one that..."

"You did it to me though, didn't you?"

I turned around to see Mary Classier, eighteen and beautiful. She held in her hand a giant, black dildo. "You did it to me, and I will do it to you." As she spoke, these words another Mary Classier stepped up to stand by the elbow of the other one, this one seven years old and adorable with a cowlick sticking up in the back. I remembered the picture of Mary looking like this younger version, but I still didn't remember messing up her hair. The girl pulled out scissors and smiled, sporting a mouthful of gaps.

I backed away as the girls started closing in. Behind them, I could see the army coming out of the darkness. My mother and father were coming for my car keys. Then another older set was coming with Christmas gifts for the year I stayed in L.A. Finally, an even older version of my mother was coming with a walker wanting an unspeakable revenge for the nursing home that she still tells me she likes. Kids, strangers, and friends all coming for some measure of revenge. Dozens of women coming to break my heart for what I did to them.

A fist struck me, and I went to my knees. I looked up to see the skinny punk I had laid out in the Testament pit at the Mississippi Knights concert in 1989. The dumb shit had been throwing elbows and had hit my girl right in the temple. I had grabbed his shoulder and dropped him. Security slapped me on the shoulder and hoisted the asshole out of the show. Two different people bought me beers for dropping the dude. I wasn't sorry for it. Not a name that should be on the wall. I was a God damned hero that night. The thought rang through my head: "a God damned hero." Then I heard the unmistakable sound and tug of my own hair being cut. Little Mary had caught me on the ground. I jumped up, ready to boot her and take on the punk again, but both were gone.

The older Mary was there though, and the dildo slapped at my suddenly naked backside. I turned toward the wall in desperation and saw Bret standing before me on the inside of the wall. His ghost hand reached toward me, and I started to shrink away when I saw that the bottle of vodka pass into my hand.

"Is this what you want? You want me to drink myself to death?"

"Yes," Mary whispered in my ear.

"Yes," cried the crowd forming around me.

My elderly mother screamed at me. "Die, you shithole!"

I started to raise the bottle to my lips when I saw Bret shaking his head. It was then that I understood. It was war strategy. I took a mouthful of the vile liquid and spat it onto the wall. I slapped my hand against the names and with a single swipe, eliminated a half dozen of my attackers. Cries of rage busted from the crowd as I splashed more of the bottle onto the wall. I watched as the words *Mary Classier sodomized* melted into runny streaks and the woman with the dildo vanished into a dark goo that seeped into the ground.

I scrubbed the wall clean of my sins, erasing even Bret with a few minutes of scrubbing. I stepped back and evaluated my handiwork. They were all gone. Then a new one that formed as I watched the wall. *Ava neglected.* Ava, my God, how could I erase Ava? I heard her crying the way she did when she was only three months old, the way she did when I moved out.

I turned toward the darkness and saw her. She was so tiny, so lovely, her petite fingers were slapping at plastic Christmas ornaments that we had hung from the handle of her pumpkin-seat. I ran to her and crouched down to look at my beautiful daughter. For her, I felt guilt. The others could all go fuck themselves, but Ava, my beautiful Ava, how could I ever have left her?

I slowly lifted the pumpkin-seat to look more closely at the little angel.

The screeching voice echoed through the darkness. "Put her down!" I knew the voice and I nearly did as she commanded out of fear. Lindsey was a ruthless woman. I sometimes wonder how I survived the divorce. Then the baby cooed, and I knew I couldn't put her down, not again, not like this. I started walking in the direction opposite of Lindsey.

"Come back here now!"

I didn't look back. I stepped up on a board and started running the length of it. I saw mud on both sides of the board and quickly stepped onto the next board and ran its length. Lindsey's voice echoed behind me. When I turned to gage my distance, I saw the heavy fog hanging in the air and a few goats stepping over the boards and sinking to their belly into the mud. I had been there before. I had been there with Lindsey. Then Lindsey came out of the fog, her hips swinging and rage on her face. She looked young and beautiful, the way she had when I had left her and Ava.

I ran. As the fog cleared and the green country and medieval architecture in the distance revealed itself I knew where I was. I cursed as I stopped on the edge of the bluff with a giant fall before me. I put Ava down and turned toward Lindsey.

"We are in Glendalough," I said to her.

"What is that supposed to mean to me?" She looked around with scorn.

"This is where she was conceived. Don't you remember? Down in the youth hostel. We took a day trip here during our Dublin vacation."

"So?"

"There's a reason we are here. There's a reason you and I are here. I need to right the wrongs I did to both of you when you were these ages. I can't erase you two. You two are my life."

She laughed, and I felt the disdain I had been feeling for her since long before Ava, since before I left. "You think you can just fix things like this? Your daughter is in high school now. She has boyfriends."

I looked at the baby in the pumpkin-seat and wished with all of my soul that I had never left her. Nothing was worth leaving her. The thought lingered, just outside of my rational mind that she

105

isn't in high school any more. She is in college. I'm paying for her college.

Then the pumpkin-seat slid on the rocks. I dove for it, but it was too late. I had lost her. She had slipped over the ledge to plummet a thousand feet into the icy blue waters of Glendalough.

Lindsey screamed and threw herself over the ledge in the direction of where Ava had slid. I grunted and launched myself over the ledge. I screamed as the wind sucked at my face, and I watched as the water drew closer. I prepared for the impact, but the impact never comes.

I'm alone.

halfway there! Tripping any?

Jake Walters
Damned Detention

Milton High School was the epicenter of their boredom and bad feelings during the day, but when night fell, and they told their mothers they were going to a friend's house. They met up in front of the old, sagging chain-link fence that ran the perimeter of their school. It became an adventure. There were three of them, all freshmen. Tall, skinny Bobby, with his braces reflecting even in the night. There was Rachel, with her dark brown hair and her pale skin and her dark eyes and soft voice. There was Kit, short for his age, often ridiculed for his droopy eyes, which, at least to the upperclassmen at Milton, gave him the appearance of being a dullard. He could not tell them that it was really a condition referred to as Congenital Myasthenia Syndrome that made him look always half-asleep, always half-in this world, half-leaving; he never told them that his mother never let him outside to play basketball, or football, even though he had a feeling that he would love playing. He could not tell them about the time she made him stay home from school for a week because he had a minor cold, all because "The doctors said you aren't well." However, he could always tell Bobby and Rachel.

They met by an old lamppost that bathed the street below in a harshly white glow. They were both already waiting for him by the time Kit saw them. "Hey, guys," he said as he approached. He saw Rachel squint into the darkness, although she knew it was he.

"What took you so long?" Bobby said. He was leaning against the pole, hands in his pockets.

"I had to convince my mom. It took some doing."

"It's all right," Rachel said. "I'm glad you could come."

Kit looked to Bobby. Bobby took his hands out of his pockets and walked toward the fence. "Well, are you guys coming?" he called back over his shoulder.

"Let's go," Rachel said. Kit followed her.

The fence, worn out though it was, presented the biggest obstacle to their entrance into the school. Bobby hurled himself over easily enough—for him it was almost like taking a big step over a molehill. Rachel struggled over but landed pertly on her feet, and then they were looking at Kit. "Help me," Kit said, reaching his hands toward them.

"Oh, Jesus," Bobby said.

"Sorry," Kit said, grabbing hold of one of the guideposts. The metal was cold against his bare palm. He climbed. He reached the top; his friends took his hands and helped him over. He knew that each day he lived, his disease would progress, and his strength would decline. He could look forward to the day when he stopped breathing, or could not chew anymore, or even go to the bathroom by himself. His mother had told him about these things; she, in turn, had learned all this from The Doctors. It was grim. It was a thing he did not speak with anybody about, not even Rachel.

They put him down on the pavement and started to move toward that the giant shadowy hulk known as Milton High School. The bricks were cold, and Kit put his hand up against the wall so that he could catch his breath. "Hang on, just a sec," he told his friends. They waited a few feet in front of him, in a pool of darkness, but he could hear Bobby breathing impatiently. "All right," he said, taking to his feet again, a few moments before he thought he was fully prepared. "Let's go."

They went on until they found an open door. They knew from previous experience that the janitors always forgot to lock at least one of the doors, and oftentimes even more. They sometimes left them even completely open, and raccoons and cats would prowl the hallways at night. Some mornings the kids saw footprints in the classrooms.

This door led into the kitchen and Kit followed his friends inside. The food preparation area was full of pots and pans hanging from the ceiling, and low counters. Kit stared at a knife left on a cutting board, some seeds and other unidentifiable foodstuffs congealed upon its blade. "I think I'll pack a lunch tomorrow," he said. There was bread, crumbling, a few feet away, and the rinds of some fruit sitting like a wild pig's meal at the zoo. They worked their way into the cafeteria proper, lit in the dull glow of emergency lights. All those tables and those round plastic stools, black, the kind that squeaked when you sat down. There was Kit's usual table, where he sat with Rachel, Bobby, and a few other misfits that sometimes emerged from study hall to eat with general society. The place stank and he wanted to leave. He had seen too much here during waking hours; the time Henry Griffith beat the hell out of another boy for allegedly saying something about his mother; the time Wendy what's-her-name got her period and walked around with blood-stained legs for the rest of the day, either unaware of what had happened to her, or too afraid to address it.

They walked into the hallway. "Can I see your hall passes, please?" Bobby said in his best Vincent Price impression.

"Shut up," Rachel said. "Don't listen to him, Kit."

At the teachers' lounge, they opened the refrigerator and dug through the food. Kit was not hungry, but Bobby pulled out what looked like a tuna fish sandwich, unwrapped it, and shoved it into his mouth. "Hey, this is pretty good," he said around the mashing foot in his mouth. "Want a bite?"

"Ew, no," Rachel said, moving toward the door. "Come on, we can't stay here all night."

"Suit yourselves," he said, tossing the remaining few bites into the trash. Kit followed them again into the hallway. They walked to the science lab, where old Mr. Yates taught Biology and Chemistry. Nobody much cared for the teacher, but nobody could exactly explain why not. The kids ducked into the classroom and looked at the dusty chalkboard. They moved about the desks. "Hey," Bobby said, "we should turn all the desks to face the other direction."

"No," Kit said. Truthfully, he thought that would be a funny prank to play on poor Mr. Yates, but he did not have the breath, or the strength, to turn that many desks.

"Kit's right," Rachel said. "Let's go. This place gives me the creeps."

They walked past a cabinet full with jawbones and pickled animals; pigs, pinkish-white, their eyes squeezed shut in hideous death-grimaces. There were snakeskins and other, unknowable bones, all ancient and forgotten. Kit wondered from where they all had come.

Outside, Kit shook himself to rid himself of an attack of the shivers.

"You all right?" Rachel asked him.

"I'm fine," he said. He wanted this disease not to stand in his way—he would ask Rachel to marry him, if he only had more time. He knew that was foolish. How many days could he possibly have left? Even now, he sometimes woke up in the morning and had to pull himself from bed the way an old woman will, squinting against the sun. No, not even that was exactly right, because he could not squint. His eyes were in a constant state of half-squinting against the outside world, sun, or moon.

Kit followed them and then he heard something. He said, "Stop," his voice barely above a whisper. Either they heard him, or they had heard the same thing he had. "Did you guys hear that?"

"What?" Bobby said, taking a few more steps forward. "Hello!" he yelled to the abandoned school. Kit listened to his voice echo down the corridor. "Anybody there? Mr. Yates?" He laughed and jammed his hands back into his pockets. "See, Kit? It's just us. Nobody else. Maybe just a rat or something."

"I swear I heard it," Kit said.

"Come on," Rachel said. "Maybe we should get out of here."

"Why?" Bobby asked. "Because Kit's afraid? This'll be good for him. Just five more minutes."

Maybe he's right, Kit thought. "Fine," he said. "Let's just be quick." They moved on through the school, past closed lockers and darkened classrooms. Their footsteps slapped down against the hallway floor and Kit could hear himself breathing. He tried to calm it. *You're with your friends*, he thought. *These people like you.*

Laughter, from some deep recess of the school. "There it is again," Kit said, halting.

"I heard it too," Rachel said, feeling out in the dark for Kit's hand and finally locating it. He grabbed on and held it.

"Maybe," Bobby said. "I think someone else might be doing the same thing we're doing."

"We should go," Kit said. "They tease us during the day when there're teachers around. What do you think they'll do to us now?" He imagined various scenarios, most involving his overnight confinement in a cramped locker, his early morning release by a pitying custodian.

"No," Bobby said. "Don't you get it, man?"

"Get what?"

"That's the reason they make fun of us. Because we're always hiding. This is our chance to make some friends. Or at least to show them that we can be cool."

Kit felt his eyelids drooping even more. It was something he was often unaware of, like his own breathing or heartbeat. Now, with some struggle, he opened his eyes wider. "I don't want to make friends with them," Kit said. "You're my friends. That's enough for me."

"Not for me," Bobby said, moving forward in the dark.

Rachel sighed. She tugged Kit onward a few steps. He knew that she never looked at herself for very long in the mirror. Sometimes when he was at her house and she caught her own reflection in the mirror, he could see her reimagining her image, building it from scratch the way other kids built forts and puzzles. But she never got the pieces down to her own satisfaction. He wondered what that mirror had witnessed; her tears, her hungry gaze. He knew that his own mirror had seen much of the same written across his own face, as he asked those unanswerable questions about why him, and why this way, and when.

He allowed her to pull him along, as he thought about her, and the things she thought about herself. If she was ugly, then there was no hope for him. They moved toward the laughter, which had died down now to a low shuffling of feet and papers and a strange smacking sound, which took Kit a few moments to realize, was bubblegum getting the business.

"Shush," Bobby said, stopping them at a corner. A strange, blue light was bleeding from beneath one of the classroom doors. "It's coming from the detention room."

Kit had never been in this room except for when he had sat down to meet with his school counselor, a fat woman named Mrs. Frederick, who looked at him sadly. His mother had been there, and she had asked question after question, an archer whose quiver was full of questions, all of her concerns addressed to the point where Kit had to inject, "Okay, Mom. They'll take care of me."

Now they crept up to the room again and, side by side, they peeked over the window set high in the door. Kit was the shortest of them and his eyes just cleared the wood, as he stood straight. Bobby had to crouch down. *Don't let them see your braces,* Kit wanted to say, and then stifled a laugh. When he saw the group inside the detention room, his sense of humor failed.

None of them was kids. The entire room looked like the wavy image a poor projector will show at the cinema, everybody bathed in a sickly blue light. Kit could hear them speaking and he watched them interact with each other. All of them were adults. There was a fat, balding man sitting in the back row with his hands interlaced on his desk, watching everybody. He was wearing a suit and his dark eyes flicked back and forth, back and forth, from student to student. Another had his shirtsleeves rolled up, his hair slicked back, and was puffing away at a cigarette. He was sitting in the middle row, but to Kit, they *all* looked like they were sitting in the back row. Another was handsome, with dark hair and a disarming smile; he looked like he might be a neighbor, or a Little League coach. One woman toward the front of the class, whom everybody seemed to refer to as Ma, had hard eyes and a straight posture. She snapped at the hooligans in back. "Quit yer yappin back there or I'll switch the lot of ya!"

"What the hell is this?" Bobby said.

Kit was frozen. He wanted to answer something, anything, but none of his muscles would move. It was not because of his condition.

One man was sitting alone. He was fat and gnawing at a nasty-looking sandwich, but he spent most of his time looking around the room, as if afraid that somebody was going to hit him. Kit realized that the fat man reminded him of himself.

Kit heard a familiar voice call on one of the pupils, Albert, to come to the board. Albert stood. He was a tall, skinny man with dark hair slicked back. He looked like an ordinary plumber, but Kit could tell that something about the man was very dangerous. "I don't know," Albert said.

The teacher responded. "Come give it a try, why don't you?" It was Mr. Yates.

"Aw," Albert said, deflating. Some of the other pupils sniggered and one of them threw a wadded up piece of paper at him. Kit watched as the paper flew through Albert's head and bounced off a desktop before coming to rest between Ma's feet. She kicked it away the way a man kicks over his spit in the dust.

"Oh my God," Kit heard Rachel whisper. "They're ghosts."

"No," Bobby said. "That's Mr. Yates."

"I'm going in," Kit said.

His friends did not hear him. They continued bantering back and forth, about what was right in front of them. In the meantime, Albert made his way to the front of the classroom and took a piece of chalk from Mr. Yates, who was standing at the desk, surveying his class. Albert stood at the board and scratched his head, and Mr. Yates told him, "Take it slow."

Kit's hand had found the doorknob of its own volition, and he turned it. He heard Bobby say, "Shit, what are you doing!" Rachel grabbed his shoulder and tried to pull him back, and under most circumstances, she would have easily done it. But not tonight. Kit walked through the door and everybody swiveled in his or her chairs to look at him. In some ways, it was not unlike all the other times he entered classrooms at Milton High. He felt like the new kid, all over again. The door slammed behind him, whether by itself or because Bobby shut it.

Mr. Yates peered at him over his spectacles. "Kit," he said. "How nice of you to join us." Kit did not respond, and so the teacher said, "Why don't you take a seat?"

Kit looked at the class. He remembered kindergarten, zigzagging his way through a chaotic room, the way the teacher hovered over him to be certain that a wayward building block did not catch him in the face, protecting him. He remembered the way kids asked him about his condition for the first couple of days, and his struggles to answer them coherently. He could not say the name—Congenital Myasthenia Syndrome—and so he stuck with CMS for those formative years. Many kids gave him an extra-wide berth in the classroom or on the playground, afraid they would catch it. Some gave him wedgies, and wet willies, and flicked the backs of his ears, and he cried. He did not want to cry, of course, but something about it felt right. His chest always heaved and sometimes he thought he was going to die right then and there, not just because of his lungs, but because everybody was staring. A few years later, he found Bobby and Rachel, and they made it easier to ignore the other kids. In fact, the three of them ignored everybody else as far as that was possible.

The guy that looked like James Dean was patting the empty chair beside him. "Come on over, kid," he said in a Midwestern accent. "What's your name?"

"I'm Kit," he answered, certain that Mr. Yates had already said that. He moved, slowly at first, aware of Ma's sharp, watchful eye. He sat down.

"What's your name?" Kit said.

"Charlie Starkweather," the guy said, puffing at his cigarette, blowing the smoke back toward the ceiling. "Nice to meet you."

"Thanks," Kit said.

"Could you keep it down?" Mr. Yates asked from the front of the room. Albert was still gazing at the blank chalkboard.

"Sorry," Kit said, but Charlie put his hand on Kit's forearm and shook his head. The cigarette dangled from his lips at such an angle that it looked about ready to fall to the floor.

"Screw off, Yates," Charlie said. Then, to Kit, he said, "Don't let no teacher tell you what to do. You understand?"

Kit nodded his head. "Who are you guys?" he asked. He turned in his chair and looked again at their faces. They were hard faces, with menacing eyes. Many of them had scars on their chins or foreheads, or strange burns on their forearms. Some of them were sweating profusely, but still they looked relaxed. They stared back at Kit, and one of them grinned; when he did, Kit shivered. These were not good people.

"These are a bunch of clowns," Starkweather said offhandedly. "A bunch of misfits and wannabes, low-lifers and two-timers. The detention crew."

"Hey, put a sock in it," a man said. Kit turned and saw a big man, one eye closed, the other looking disdainfully at them. "I'm tryin to learn something."

"Cram it, Lucky," Starkweather said.

"I'll cram you," Lucky said, standing. He was tall and wore a wristwatch; suddenly Kit wanted very badly to know what time it read, but he did not dare move.

"Get up, kid," Starkweather mumbled down toward him. "Get up!"

Kit stood. Lucky looked down at both of them. One was just a little kid with droopy eyes and a nervous twitch. The other was another kid, but bigger, probably big enough to hurt somebody. Definitely big enough to hurt somebody. Kit could smell a strange cologne wafting off his body. It reminded him of formaldehyde. "You're tough, huh?" Lucky said.

"There ain't no families no more," Starkweather said. "We're all on our own. So you want to go, we're gonna go."

Lucky looked back and forth again, from one to the other, and Kit did not know how much longer he could stand there, trying not to shiver. He heard a rough woman's voice from behind. "Sit down, the lot of ya. I'll send you all back to hell." It was Ma, and, incredibly, both men sat, saying things like *excuse me* and *sorry, ma'am.*

Kit stood in the room for another moment, and then he saw Starkweather looking up at him. Between puffs of his cigarette, he said, "You did good, kid. Real good."

Then they were gone. All of them. The men, Ma, Mr. Yates. Kit looked at the board, hoping to see some half-solved math problem there, Albert's work, but there was nothing. Just a blank, dusty board. "Hello?" he said weakly. Nobody answered.

Kit moved as fast as he could to get out of the classroom, expecting the door to have locked. He almost burst into tears of joy when it swung freely open. "Rachel! Bobby!" he called down the hallway. They were gone. He retraced their steps through the hallways, the echoes of their voices still ringing in his mind. *They were dead. They were real.* He worked his way through the cafeteria and the kitchen, bumping into tables and counters, not caring. He found the door easily enough and it opened for him without his even having to exert much force in opening it. The night air was cold and hit him like an ocean wave, and instantly he knew it had all been an illusion.

Kit walked near the wall of the school and a few moments later almost tripped over Rachel. She was sitting against the wall, and she jumped up when Kit came. "Oh," she said, hugging him. "Oh, Kit."

"Where's Bobby?" he asked her.

She moved her face back and took his in her hands. "Forget about him. He went home. I'm so glad you made it out safe." She was crying. He hugged her back, feeling like he had a new source of strength.

"Come on," he told her. "We should go."

"What happened back there?" she asked him.

"Detention," he said.

The next day, the school was warm and open again. Light shone where the night before had been only shadow; the detention room, which Kit walked very slowly and cautiously by, was empty, and everything was in its rightful place. At home the previous evening, after parting with Rachel in front of his house, he had looked up Charlie Starkweather. Pictures had flashed on the screen almost instantly, and it was he. Charlie. Kit read what Starkweather did: the gas station attendant, the girlfriend's parents, the little two-year-old clubbed to death in her bed. All the other victims across Nebraska, into Wyoming, eventually getting strapped into the electric chair and fried into the next world; or, Kit supposed, into detention.

Kit had taken special notice of Starkweather's childhood. His thick glasses, his speech problems. Other kids made fun of him. *He's just like me*, Kit thought, and then banished the idea away. Never.

He met with Rachel in front of their lockers. "Where's Bobby?" he asked her.

"Sick today," she said, looking down at her feet. They both knew it was a lie.

Kit felt somebody staring at him, and when he turned, he saw a small pocket of sophomores looking his way. One of them smiled and said, "Hey, you gotta girlfriend, Droopy?" Kit looked at Rachel and saw her face turning red. He considered the company he shared the night before—a class full of not just bad kids, but the worst kids. These bullies meant little to him now.

He started to walk toward them and shook off Rachel's hand as she tried to stay him. He walked directly at them and watched as they unfolded their group of football players and underachievers for him. He did not know what he was going to do, even as he approached. Maybe say something like *shut the hell up,* or something more vulgar. He went directly to the one that had called him Droopy.

"Were you talking to me?" he asked.

"That's right," the other said, starting to laugh.

Kit pulled back his fist and swung as hard as he could. His punch landed squarely on the bully's nose, and he cried out and grabbed for his face. Already blood was starting to pour out, and he was looking at his hands as if he could not believe what he was seeing. Kit heard murmurs of "Holy shit," and much of the foot traffic in the corridor had stopped to witness this strange event. Already, Rachel was at his side, pulling him back. He knew punishment awaited, and he knew what that likely meant: detention. As long as it was not with Mr. Yates, he could handle it. He backed away, staring at the group of bullies who had crossed him. He felt like his eyes were wide open.

Variation on John D. Stanton's cover art

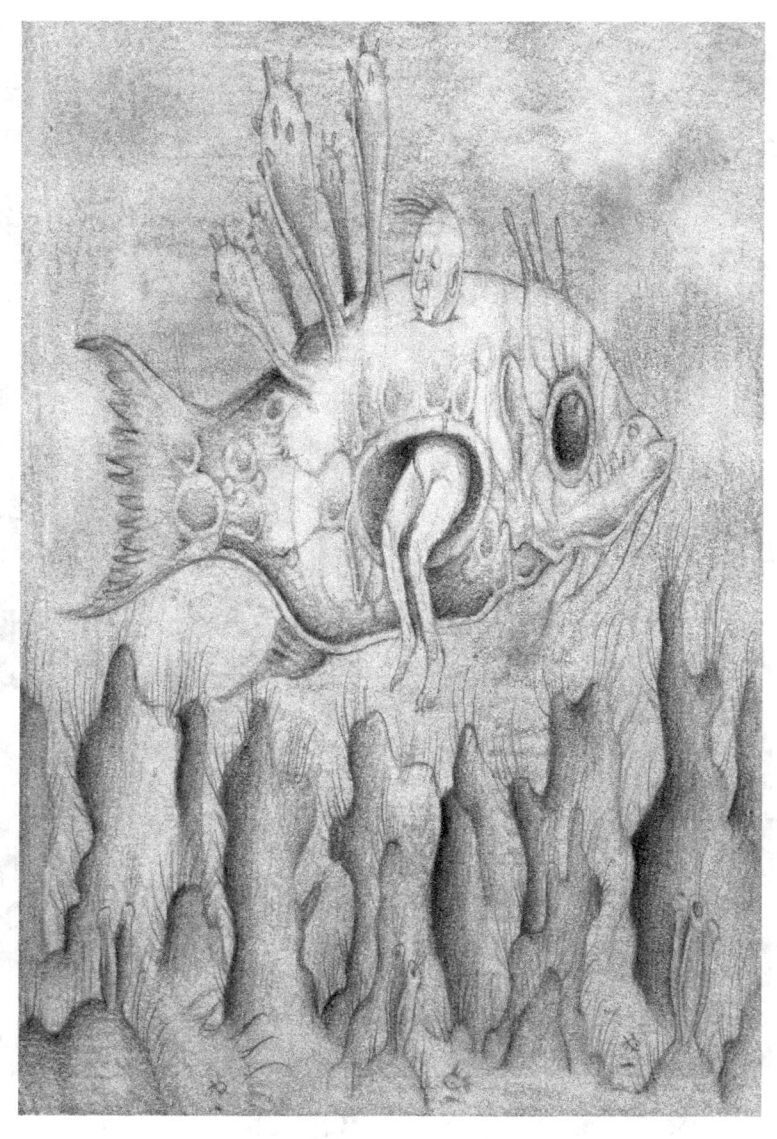

J.C. Burkart
back back, monster, I Hold Fire!

LiarrrLieeeWannntttLikkke
YouuuWannnttt   runs out
the full blast bathtub tap.
What Will You Do,
What About You   is the over-
flow drain, a hidden mouth
gulping in waste water beneath
an upturned nose   stopper lever.

One eye a Flathead and the other
Phillips   cartoons   one dead
and one alive   quenched chrome fixture.

You endure a distorted nude man
more knees than balls on your face.

What Will You Do, What-About-You?

One more displacement smothered
you   elemental   still asking those guttural questions.

Good for you! you dilate no further,
to get at you takes two different tools
applied to cat and one dead eye.

Make a man work for it   cover
his hands in grime
of an inner snake.
Give back the dead
skin gray and green
and orange   black the live palms
that seek to re-gut you,
once liquid in mechanized fires.

What will you do,
what about
you, interrupted ghost throat?

No   NotNotNot   the gift
from faucet drips.

A hand can turn on *LiarrrLieeeYouuuWannnttt*   like fire,

like forgetting   like not knowing
where shitten waste water goes.

Wash cloth over eyes   Hell's Fire!
A man should give a damn, re-meet a hovering
Hairy Monster   lie teller,

maker of a little liar   scab picker   washer
of cloth wet with thrown fire.
WannnnttttLlllikeeeYou Wannnttt   the knob on
full blast by hands
that enter nothing
without a drawing
back   without hesitation.

J.C. Burkart
my One-Eyed white Dishwasher

steam calls out for melody

NeverWasYouNeverWere
NeverWasYouNeverWere
                              Yet
the plate
clinks against a twin
a house made of bamboo and Asian women in blue
on the two of you
                    Yet
                    unlike long dead bards and courtesans
                    grins glaze over porcelain lucky enough
                    to rub away
                    to not contact an angry floor—
NeverWasYouNeverWere
NeverWasYouNeverWere
                    Yet
singer near, pinned to the floor—*NeverWas*—reflection-less,
lucky rubbed,
bottom opened, made still—*YouNeverWere*—
                    Yet
filled up by a woolly grip—*NeverWas*—boy believed he felt
bamboo—
YouNeverWere—filled in your rear—
                    Yet
he was told to and not to tell—
                    Yet
he sang and laughed because
your offspring know and because
you knew an other too.

J.C. Burkart

Old Flip-phone in My Toilet

DooYoouWannaGooooOn?
            Kinda.
            Kinda.
There's no sleep in the eyes
in the yellow mirror and the forehead
is a bubbling blur. How many times
was a .38 between them? How many
times was it bravery stepping up
sleepless in front of easy terror.

Time to go again:
DooYoouWannaGooooOn?
            Kinda.
            Kinda.
Going straight is money and life trickling in and out in waves.
Not tossing bodies or having been tossed in that restless
Reservoir, Beaver Lake.
Who can't love a mocking thing?
Who can't love a stone embankment that never learned how to
laugh and said
goback-goback-away-goback

                        all damned night?

Weights on the legs and arms bound,
the best baptism, but the money came through, who doesn't love
a bailout by the big man's great hand that closed a silver book of
life and thumbed down
its antenna for a pen?

My cast off particulates, and probably piss, would've become one
with everyone who drank from a tap. Bigg'un found his
Benjamins.
Now there's a dream. My old friends hang me off a listing boat,
there's waking up
bald and afraid. What happens now that there's no being
flushed, and ankles go stiff in the night when I pee?

DooYoouWannaGooooOn?
  Kinda.
  Kinda.

J.C. Burkart
as if the raven Mask and I were never There

Exploding, it's always the downstairs neighbors.
Three snake skins pinned behind a glass picture frame hit the—
                    —Birrd!
The face of man over diamond skins has stopped trembling.
There is a child, a boyfriend, and a girlfriend below
who have an identical wall next to a door where they, reflected
might—
                    —Birrdd!
In a call to flight, scales, progenitors of feathers,
burst beyond lamplight and human glasses
which had been on a child, boyfriend—
                    —Thatt
is all the Mardi Gras mask can say, mounted, broken feathered,
a pithy said all day from behind, in porcelain rapport.
Who could conceal—
                    —You Prickless Bastard!
we think the wall said, a child giving up on flight—
                    —Thatt! thattt
again the cracked
eyeless skinless mask,
and scales and glass,
a floor as fireworks.
Confetti.

J.C. Burkart
They stole my Where Are My Kids?

Can't listen to a dial tone to fall asleep
on the precipice of the talking brain-rot   dementia
found a ledge below the jumped off ledge
and speak the meanderings of just hatched mind-worms
mouth out the interrupted
grooves and tell of the new corn mash
brain Stihl flipped over
and enemy everyone   which is everyone   pined for
fretted over is gone   for this instant.   An old person is crying
above a rotary phone call
on the vanity a cloudy day

hangs

over the right-hand

shoulder.
Who is not out that window for me to miss anymore?
Doooonot-not-not-not-not-not-Not-Not...

Tom Howard
The Pond

Out of the corner of his eye, Manny saw the small shadow dart down the hallway.

"Did you brush your teeth?" he called.

"Yeah," his grandson said from his room.

"Today?"

The silence that followed told Manny all he needed to know. Retired, Manderly Horton never expected he'd be caring for his deceased son's nine-year-old. The boy's father, a single parent, had killed himself and left the child alone in the world. Manderly, called Manny by his family, remained the only responsible adult the boy had.

"Brush your teeth. I'm going to check afterwards."

Silas muttered something Manny felt fortunate he couldn't hear. The widower had raised four children and had looked forward to spending his afternoons fishing from the dock with the other old men. However, he couldn't tell the authorities to send the boy to a foster home. Manny felt guilty he hadn't been in better touch with his disturbed son, a depressed man who drank too much and never held a steady job. Silas, the reticent child, arrived with a backpack and not much else. Tall and thin, the dark-headed boy proved difficult from the beginning. The boy didn't sleep, only ate sweets, and didn't listen to anything Manny said. Silas had little parental control growing up. His mother had disappeared in the middle of the night, leaving the infant alone with his harried father.

Manny tried hard to make him part of his family. The boy avoided hugs and any signs of affection. Manny, exhausted and dismayed when his little house was trashed by the end of the day, considered spanking his grandson although he'd never physically punished his own children.

Not hearing the sound of running water from the bathroom, Manny pushed himself out of his recliner and went to check. He found Silas scrubbing the inside of the toilet bowl with the old man's toothbrush.

Manny resisted the urge to strangle the child. "I guess you didn't want me to drive you to the skateboard park in the morning. Brush your teeth and go to bed. If you kick another hole in the wall, we'll never go to the skate park again. Do you understand?"

The boy stuck his chin out but nodded. Manny had learned he could discipline the boy by removing things he treasured, things like visits to the park across town.

When he returned to his recliner, Manny tried to convince himself Silas meant no harm. He didn't hurt anyone on purpose. He couldn't help it if he'd grown up high-spirited and undisciplined. A disastrous dinner with friends ended when Silas made a mess of his food and crawled under the table. Manny paid the bill and took him home.

"What is wrong with you?" Manny had demanded when they got in the car.

"I'm bored," said the boy, his blue eyes cold. "Can we go do something fun?"

"Not after the way you acted today. I'm ashamed to take you out of the house."

"You hate me, don't you?" The boy lowered his head. "Everybody does."

Manny's felt a twinge of guilt. "No, I don't hate you. But you make it difficult sometimes."

"I'm sorry," Silas said. "Can we go somewhere?"

Manny had shaken his head and sent Silas outside to play when they returned home. He'd considered sending the young hellion to his room, but Manny hadn't yet plastered over the holes Silas had kicked in the walls last time.

"What am I going to do with him," Manny asked his sister the morning after the toothbrush incident. She proved one of the few people brave enough to visit since Silas's arrival.

Gabby sat down her cup of coffee and shook her head. "There's something missing from that boy, Manny. He's going to end up in prison or worse if you don't do something."

"He can't help it," said Manny. "First his mom ran off, then his dad killed himself. He's barely nine. The only way he's survived this long is to be belligerent and defensive."

"Imagine what he's going to be like as a teenager," she said, glancing at the door. "He'll kill somebody."

Manny sighed. "I don't know what to do, Gabby. He won't listen to me. He bangs around the house at all hours of the night. Thank goodness I hid the matches."

"I remember another kid with a dark streak," said Gabby.

"I was never as bad as that."

"I remember the time Mama caught you spitting in a cat's eye before you threw it off the roof. That's when she first threatened you with the pond."

"The pond," repeated Manny, barely suppressing a shudder. "I would never subject anyone to that."

"After all the scary stories Grandma told us about the creatures who lived down there, we didn't expect you back when Daddy tossed you in. We were scared to death they'd keep you, but you surfaced immediately."

"I couldn't do that to Silas. I still have nightmares. You think I visited there for a few minutes, but for me, it seemed like months in hell. I don't want to talk about it." The horrible things he'd seen and had done to him on the other side hadn't faded over the years.

Gabby shook her head. "Okay, but when Silas pokes some kid's eye out or sets your house on fire, you'll wish you had." She rose and gave him a hug. "If Silas lived with me, I wouldn't hesitate to take him to the old pond."

Manny stared into space. "I couldn't let him go through alone."

"Grandma said if you went in twice, you stayed there," said Gabby. "You can't go with him. Throw him in and let him be responsible for himself for a change. You came out a better person."

"I can't," Manny said. "I never forgave Dad for sending me there."

She hugged him again and left with her coffee unfinished.

One foggy morning, Manny had had enough. He awoke with a heavy heart about his decision and went to Silas's room to watch him as he lay sleeping. The boy had taken to curling up in the closet in an old sleeping bag. The old man had quickly learned which battles were worth fighting and which were not. Let the kid sleep in the closet while a perfectly comfortable bed sat two feet away. He shook the boy awake and told him to come to breakfast.

Manny, hating himself for what he had planned prepared the boy his favorite – pancakes with syrup – and didn't yell when Silas refused to use his silverware. They hadn't been speaking much since Silas beat up the little Nichols kid next door and broke his arm. Manny wasn't as concerned about having to pay for the doctor bills on his fixed income as he was about Silas's lack of remorse.

Manny had reached the end of his rope, and that gave him an idea. With school looming nearer and nearer, Manny had to break his own promise of never returning to the pond, of never subjecting anyone to the horror waiting on the other side.

He convinced himself that Silas would be all right if Manny lowered him into the pond for only a few seconds. Manny would tie a rope to the boy and pull him back up immediately. Maybe the kid would see how well he had it if he experienced a few minutes of real terror.

Manny swallowed his guilt and tied the old aluminum canoe on the top of his car. He placed the paddles and rope in the back seat.

Silas, wearing the clothes he'd worn all week and freshly christened with syrup from breakfast, squinted at the canoe in the early-morning light. "Are we going fishing, Manny?" He refused to call the old man grandpa.

"No," said Manny. "I need you to find something for me. Get in the car."

As the car bounced along the gravel road to the top of the mountain, Manny said, "I haven't been up here in years. My family used to live up here."

Silas turned from the window and asked, "What am I going to get for you?"

"You'll see," said Manny, searching for the farm lane leading to his family's old house. He couldn't believe how much the brush had grown up. Since the city had bought the land for a watershed, not many people visited the old homestead.

Manny asked, "You're not chicken, are you?"

Silas's chin shot out. "Don't call me that, asshole."

"Watch your mouth. A little cold water won't hurt you a brave boy like you."

Silas gave him a suspicious look, but Manny could see him calculating what he'd get in trade for doing Manny a favor.

Plants and small trees clogged the lane, but Manny got close enough to unload the canoe and hand Silas the rope. "To pull you back up," Manny explained.

The old pond hadn't changed. Lurking under the cedars, it felt stale and unwholesome. Clumps of tadpole eggs and algae floating on the surface. Half the size of a football field, the pond lay unused for fishing or swimming. Aside from Manny's being thrust beneath the surface, he couldn't remember anyone being brave enough to dip a toe in it.

Silas made a face as they stood on the bank. "It stinks. What is down there?"

"A chest my family hid on the bottom," lied Manny, slipping the canoe into the noxious water. "Maybe we'll go to the video arcade afterwards."

"Some kind of treasure?" Silas looked excited. "I'm a good swimmer."

"Yes, but don't jump in until I get to the middle of the pond and tie the rope around you. It will be cold and dark down there."

"I'm not afraid," Silas asserted.

That will change. "Good," said Manny, rowing them out.

"I didn't bring my swimsuit," said Silas, trying to peer into the dark waters beneath them.

"Your clothes will be fine," said Manny, tying the rope around the boy's thin chest. "You won't be down long. Are you ready?"

Silas nodded and slid out of the canoe into the water.

"Remember," said Manny with a catch in his voice, "go to the bottom, and bring the chest right back up."

Silas held his nose and let go of the side of the canoe, quickly sinking out of sight.

As Manny sweated and counted to ten, images of Silas's future victims kept him from pulling the boy up too soon. Ten seconds on the other side should be long enough to teach the boy to be a human being. He pulled in the rope, surprised at how little Silas weighed. When the frayed end of the rope appeared, Manny realized his plan had gone horribly wrong.

He'd stranded the boy on the other side.

Without thinking, Manny tore off his windbreaker and jumped into the water, returning to the other side of the pond for the second and final time.

His heart pounding, Manny struggled to reach the bottom. The water fought him, wrapping him in liquid as thick as molasses. The darkness and the cold pushed him back, but he pressed on. When he burst through the other side, spewing foul-tasting water from his laboring lungs, he searched for Silas. He ignored childhood memories of the terrors lurking in the skeletal trees and struck out for shore.

Manny saw no sign of the boy. Time moved differently on this side of the pond, and most likely Silas had already landed in trouble. Manny dragged himself out of the oily water under the overcast sky and caught his breath. A great wall stood in the distance, separated from the pond by a massive forest of dead trees.

Something rustled in the underbrush, and Manny hid behind a thorn bush as three creatures from his childhood nightmares scrambled to the edge of the water and sniffed the ground. Shaggy and naked, they looked like balding orangutans with pasty complexions and slumped shoulders. Fangs he remembered too well protruded from their human-like faces. With a snarl, the largest creature turned and ran into the dark forest, and the others followed. They must be returning to their camp.

As he stood to follow, something struck him in the stomach. He fell to the moldy ground. A small woman stood over him with her spear held high.

"Where are you going, wildling?" she asked, prodding Manny with her spear.

"I'm no—" Manny looked down at himself. He had short, well-muscled legs, long arms, and a covering of gray hair. The clothing he'd worn when he'd jumped in the pond had disappeared. Now he stood naked and looked like... "No!" He'd become one of them, one of the loathsome creatures inhabiting this nightmare land. His grandmother had been right.

Ignoring the stranger, Manny cursed the pond, the unholy magic that had brought him here and himself for killing Silas.

"Damn it," said the small woman, barely a foot tall. "You're a returnee. You're not one of them yet. I should do you a favor and kill you now."

Manny stood slowly, his fur still dripping from the pond. "They have my grandson. Do you know where they've taken him?"

"I avoid the wild ones," she said, lowering her spear. "But yes, I saw them take him." Although she stood no taller than Silas, her face and body revealed someone more mature. Her pointed ears and arched brows told him she was not human.

"I've got to save him," insisted Manny.

"You're crazy. It's too late. If you have been here before, you know what those animals do to strangers."

Manny's memories flashed back to the pain and hopelessness he'd experienced at the hands of the wildlings. At first, after the lashing and torture, he feared dying, but as the days wore on, and he regenerated each night, he prayed he would die. No matter how much of him they chewed away, every morning he awoke whole and complete. Only by eventually slipping away and throwing himself into the pond had he been able to escape."

Now the brutes had his grandson. "I have to save him." He growled and the forest woman stepped back, bumping into a hollow log.

"You can't go alone," she said.

"If you help me, I'll return you to your home."

"You don't know anything about me or my home. I can't go through the pond like you."

"I'm not talking about the pond," said Manny. "I know you're a Xex from the other side of the wall. What's a tree elf doing in a world where all the trees are dead?"

She glanced in the distance at the black wall to the west. "I wanted to see the other side of the wall. Now I'm trapped here."

"I may know a way," said Manny. "You can return to Dreamland. Help me save my grandson."

"You lie, old man!" she shouted. "You can go to the wildling's cave if you want. I'm not going to help."

"Wait!" said Manny "I have a plan. We'll use a hollow log to scare off the wildlings." The Xex looked skeptical but followed him down the path.

In a large clearing before the entrance of the cave, dozens of wildlings danced around a fire. In the middle of the bonfire stood a post. Silas hung from black vines and screamed as the flames grew. Manny froze as horrible memories filled his head. He knew how helpless and confused Silas felt.

Manny turned to the elf. "Find a dead tree that's hollow and hit it with the end of your spear. Slowly."

"Do you plan to attract them to me while you save your grandson?"

"No," said Manny, "the only things that scare wildlings are ogres." He gestured, and she thumped of the spear against the tree. "Again," he said.

The wildlings stopped in their tracks, looking toward the forest where Manny and the Xex hid in the shadows. Low grumblings of fear came from the creatures. In spite of Silas's cries of pain, they ignored him as they fled.

"It's working!" Manny exclaimed. "They think they hear the footsteps of an ogre approaching."

The wildlings had barely disappeared into the forest when Manny ran to Silas.

The boy, seeing what probably looked like another tormentor rushing at him, struggled against his bonds.

Manny pulled the burning branches from beneath Silas and sliced the vines holding the boy with his claws. A fierce growl rumbled in his chest, and he lifted Silas over his shoulder and ran back to the woods. Silas, still shouting, pummeled the old man's back.

The Xex was already on the move. "Where are we going?" Manny panted as he followed her through the dead trees. "We need to take the boy back to the pond."

"No time," said the Xex. "The wildlings are already coming back. They'll head to the pond to make sure he doesn't escape."

"Then where?" he asked. Silas had stopped shouting and was listening to their conversation.

"Spirex's lair," she replied.

Manny stopped. "We can't go there! She's more dangerous than the wildlings."

"Come on," insisted the Xex. "Madame Spider has been dead for years, but the wildlings still fear her smell. We'll be safe there until they tire of searching for your grandson."

Silas scrambled down. "Your grandson? Manny, is that you?"

"We'll talk about it when we get where we're going," said Manny. "Follow the girl."

"You're bossy enough to be Manny." Silas went around him and caught up with the Xex.

"Not for long," she said, giving Manny a smile. "By this time tomorrow, he'll be mindless and howling with the other beasts."

"What's she talking about?" asked Silas. His singed bangs were already starting to grow back, but his face remained dirty and marked with soot.

"Nothing," said Manny. "As soon as the wildlings calm down, you're going back in the pond. It'll take you home, and you'll forget all about this place."

"Did you forget?" asked the Xex.

"Shut up," barked Manny.

Spirex's lair – a giant sack of cobwebs constructed by the gigantic spider – remained where he remembered it. He trembled as he climbed the ladder behind the others. The last time he'd been in the lair, he'd barely escaped with his life.

The cocoon smelled dusty but contained enough room to be comfortable. Someone, possibly the Xex, had tossed out the

135

bones and litter. Although springy, the sack connected securely to the giant trees surrounding it.

"Are you okay?" Manny asked, placing his clawed hand on Silas's shoulder.

The boy jerked away. "I'm fine. Where are we?"

"This is where the story gets good," said the Xex. "Come on, Grandpa. Tell him what he did that that was so bad you had to send him here. Or did someone else throw him in the pond, and you just happened to jump in to save him?"

"Is that true, Manny?" Silas scowled. "What is this place?"

Manny stood and looked out the small opening. In the distance, he could hear the howls of frustrated wildlings. "I don't know. I always called it Nightmareland. It's the place my granny said they sent bad kids."

"Bad kids like me?" Silas asked.

"And me," said Manny. "I survived here for what seemed like years. My father threw me in the pond after I broke my little brother's leg. I meant for you just to see the other side, not become a victim of the wildlings. I'm sorry."

Silas looked at his bare arm, exposed through his tattered shirt. "They burned me." He lifted up his shirt. "They stabbed me. Why am I okay?"

"Brains run in the family, I see," said the Xex, reaching for her spear. "I'm going to find something to eat."

No one said anything as the small woman left the cocoon.

Silas tugged Manny's beard. "What happened to you?"

"It's a long story," said Manny. "The most important thing is to get you home."

Silas watched the Xex through the doorway. "What is she?"

"She's a wood elf," explained Manny. "Did you notice the wall out there?"

Silas nodded.

"She's from the other side. I called it Dreamland when I arrived. Dragons and happy, shiny creatures live there. Apparently overly curious elves also inhabit it."

"Can she get back?" asked Silas.

"I promised her I'd help her find a way home. I will after you are home and safe."

Silas grabbed his arm. "Is it true what she said about you having to stay behind? Are you going to send me back alone?"

"I'm sorry, Silas. You can't stay here, and I can't go back." Manny looked down at himself. "Already I can feel the wildness affecting me."

"No!" shouted Silas. "You can't leave me. Everyone leaves me. I'll be good. I promise."

Manny, surprised to see tears in the boy's eyes, said, "Silas, I love you too much to make you stay here. What you experienced is just the beginning of what the wildlings will do to you. And I'll be one of them, unable to stop myself."

Silas wiped his eyes. "She could help."

"She's helped us enough. In the morning, you're going home."

"Can you really help the elf?" Silas asked.

"Yeah," said a voice from the doorway. "Can you really help the poor stupid elf who didn't listen when they told her not to go over the wall?" The Xex opened her bag and dumped the mushrooms she'd gathered. "Don't bother with me, old man. Get your grandson home."

Manning stood. "Any sign of the wildlings?"

"They're everywhere. I've never seen them so angry."

"We'd better spend the night here and get the boy out in the morning," said Manny and reached for a mushroom. He handed it to Silas. "There should still be enough of me left in the morning to say good-bye. Thank you, Miss Xex, for the food."

Silas chewed his portion. "Yes, thank you," he mumbled.

"So," she said, reclining and eating some mushrooms, "how would you get us over the wall?"

"Last time I was here, I had a desperate plan to use the deadfall at Dead Man's Bluff."

"That is desperate. You intended to push the deadfall across the chasm and up against the wall? The bluff overlooks the deepest canyon on our side. If you fell, even someone who regenerates would be stuck in a pit for eternity."

"I was desperate," said Manny.

"You're too heavy now to make it over without help," said the Xex. "It would take someone lighter to make their way across the deadfall and secure it at the top."

"I was smaller then," said Manny with a grin. "You'll have to go."

"No," she said. "Who will hold off the wildlings when they see what we're doing?"

"She's right," said Silas. "I'll go up and tie the top of the tree to the wall."

"Absolutely not," said Manny. "You're going home first thing in the morning."

"She helped save me," said Silas. "Maybe we can go with her and go home, too."

Manny touched Silas's cheek. "You're sure you're not being reckless?"

"No. I won't go back by myself."

"It might work," said the Xex. "We knock the deadfall across the bluff and send the boy over with a coil of vines. When he reaches the top, the old man and I'll run across."

Manny didn't like the idea of keeping the boy here for one minute longer than necessary, but Silas had his chin out. Aside from knocking the boy in the head and tossing him in the pond, Manny didn't see any other option. "Go to sleep, and we'll discuss it in the morning."

"I'll take first watch," said the Xex.

"No," said Manny, watching Silas stretch out beside him. "I don't think I'll be sleeping much. This may be my last night as myself."

Silas reached for the old man's hand and gave it a squeeze before rolling onto his side and shutting his eyes.

From the doorway, Manny watched the sunrise sluggishly over Nightmare land. He might be imagining things, but the colors looked brighter, the smells stronger. His muscles weren't even sore from running with Silas over his shoulder the day before.

"Grandpa?" asked Silas as he stirred. "Do you see them?"

"No. They made a lot of noise during the night but have calmed down now. You'd better wake the girl. If we're going to try to escape through Dreamland, we need to get started."

Manny found a sturdy branch to use as a club, and the party made its way to the deadfall near the wall.

"Why didn't you use the deadfall to escape when you were here?" asked Silas, trying out several sticks to use as his own club.

"I escaped from the wildlings several times. The last time, I fell into the pond by accident and wound up home. I never suspected I could get out the way I got in. My father never told me."

"How did you plan to knock it over?" asked the Xex.

"I hadn't thought that far," said Manny. "If we're lucky, it'll be rotten at the base, and we can push it over."

"Silas," said Manny, "stop hitting things. We need to be quiet."

"Yes, Grandpa."

The deadfall showed no sign of rot. Like the other lifeless trees in the dark forest, this tree died long ago. Its tall white skeleton stood tall and overlooked the forest and the nearby chasm. After he thumped the trunk with his club, it sounded solid through and through.

Silas pointed out, "It's not rotten."

"I see that, Grandson. We need to come up with another plan. Miss Xex, do you have a way to make fire?"

She shook her head, but Silas sheepishly pulled a box of waterproof matches from his pocket. "Will these help?"

Manny took the matches. He should have checked to make sure his camping supplies were secure too.

"The wildlings will see the smoke," warned the Xex.

"Yes," said Manny, gathering small branches and placing them around the base of the tree. "We'll have to hope they don't spot it until too late. Silas, you're going to need a bigger stick."

Without gasoline, the fire started small and slowly crept up the trunk. After what seemed like hours, the charred tree trunk still didn't budge when Manny pushed against the tree with all his strength. The thicket nearby rustled, and two wildlings jumped out at them. Manny roared at them. He struck out with his club, hitting both wildlings and knocking them to the ground.

"Grandpa!" shouted Silas. "Stop!"

Manny raised his bloody club. He'd been beating first one wildling and then the other when they were both already dead. With a snarl, he broke away and stood ready for another attack.

"Let's try some of that rage on the deadfall," suggested the Xex.

Manny attacked the tree, straining with muscles he didn't know he had. The tree gave a little, then more. Silas and the Xex stood back as it lost its ancient footing and fell toward the chasm.

"I'll get the vines," said Silas before the tree had smashed against the wall. He gathered up the dark ivy and joined the Xex at the base of the trunk.

"Be careful," Manning told him.

Silas nodded and climbed the white skeleton toward the wall.

Manny looked at the chasm. "Maybe dancing around the bonfire with the old gang won't be so bad."

The Xex chuckled. "After he reaches the top, he'll have no problem securing the tree to the blocks there."

Manny didn't answer, too busy watching Silas climb the tree. Nimble as a monkey, he had almost reached the top.

It was too late. Manny hefted his club. "I can smell them coming. A large group."

"I'll take care of them," said the Xex, lifting her spear. "You start up the tree. Your grandson is finished. It should be safe."

"No. You'll never survive."

She smiled. "We'll see."

"I see wildlings coming!" shouted Silas, scurrying back down the tree.

"Stay up there," ordered Manny, but Silas slid down the truck, paying no attention to the chasm yawning below.

Growling noises from the underbrush distracted Manny, and Silas joined him with his stick ready.

Manny answered the growls with one of his own. "Xex, get up the tree. Take Silas with you."

"No," said Silas. "I'm staying. Good-bye, Miss Xex. Good luck."

"I can't leave you here," she said. The roaring noises were becoming louder.

"Go!" Manny and Silas shouted together.

"We'll catch up with you," lied Manny.

Dark birds, complaining of the disturbance in the forest, took to the air. The ground shook with the approach of countless bloodthirsty wildlings.

The Xex, looking unhappy, passed her spear to Silas. "Good luck." She disappeared up the tree.

"If they overwhelm us," said Manny. "Make your way to the pond. It's how I escaped last time."

Manny roared at the approaching wildlings as they broke through the brush.

"Go!" he shouted as he rushed the creatures. "Don't wait for me."

Silas grabbed Manny's hand and pulled him away from the wildlings and toward the pond.

Manny's instincts told him to stand and fight, but the need to protect his grandson won out, and they ran through the thorn bushes and away from the wildling horde.

They reached the shoreline, but Manny stopped at the water's edge. "I can't go with you, Silas. I can't go back."

The wildlings, unwilling to go near the water, clumped together, snarled, and thumped the ground.

"How do you know?" asked Silas. "Nobody is supposed to go back to Dreamland, either, but the elf did. I won't leave you here." Before Manny could argue, Silas grabbed his wrist and pulled him into the pond.

Manny swallowed a big gulp of foul-tasting water and tried to pull away from Silas, but the boy had wrapped his skinny arms and legs tightly around the old man. Manny couldn't break free no matter how hard he struggled. The water tugged at him, trying to separate him from his grandson, but Silas, wiry and strong, refused to let go. Some force jerked Manny violently, and he felt the boy's grip loosen and pull away.

Manny fought for the surface, certain he'd never see Silas again, but when he finally sucked in clean air, Silas treaded water beside him. Manny sputtered, surprised to see the blue sky overhead.

"We made it!" exclaimed Silas with a big grin. "We're home."

"Yes," said Manny. "Paddle for the shore."

They staggered through the reeds to firmer ground.

Plopping down beside his grandson, the old man looked out at the stagnant body of water.

"I'm sorry," said Manny. "I sent you to the other side, but I didn't intend to leave you very long. Please don't hate me." He remembered his lifelong unwillingness to forgive his father for doing exactly the same to him.

Silas turned to him. "You came for me, even though you knew what waited on the other side. You thought you couldn't come back."

Manny smiled. "I couldn't leave you to suffer like I did. Thank you for not leaving me there."

"I couldn't come back alone," said Silas.

"Maybe I should have this pond filled in," said Manny, putting his arm around the boy's shoulders.

"I don't know, Grandpa," said Silas. "I might need it someday if my grandson is a pain in the...butt."

Manny hugged Silas, and the boy didn't pull away. "I can't argue with that. Let's go home."

Calvin Demmer

The Small Hours Broadcast

"Did you hear that?" Carmen said, raising herself up against the headboard. The comforter crept down to her waist.

She received no reply.

Each passing second in the pitch-black room caused her breath to quicken. Her eyes scanned the bedroom, seeking any trace of light to verify her surroundings. After a few swings of her head, she discovered the alarm clock's digits and their glow. She focused on the shapes around the clock and made out a few items, a framed photo of her and her husband, Michael, her hairdryer, and a vase that held no flowers.

She whispered, "Hey, honey. Wake up, I heard something."

Again, she received no reply. She reached out and shook his left shoulder, keeping on until a familiar groan broke the silence.

Michael said, "What? It's late, babe."

"I heard a noise, sounded like someone . . . well, it sounded like someone tapping something in the living room, I think."

Michael took too long to reply, and Carmen shook his shoulder again.

"Stop shaking me. I'm trying to listen. Good grief, did you see the time?"

Carmen had not registered the time. She focused on the alarm clock. It was thirty-six minutes past one. Shaking her head, she thought, *who cares what time it is?*

She said, "For the third time, do you hear anything?"

"Yeah, yeah, the dripping, it's just the shower. You know it does that sometimes. I must've forgotten to close it properly. No reason to get bent out of shape over it."

"No, it's not that, Michael. I heard a different tapping sound and it didn't come from the bathroom."

"Okay, okay, I'm listening again."

As she waited, Carmen clenched her thumbs into tight balled fists, hoping he would hear the foreign sound when it returned and would take care of the problem—no matter how silly it turned out to be.

The tapping sound returned. It was as clear as any sound Carmen had heard in her existence.

"There, there," she whispered.

"Carmen, I don't hear anything."

I can't believe he's being such a dick, she thought. Her shoulders tensed as if two claws had grasped them. She fought against a wave of tears that wanted to break out and breathed in deep. When able to speak, she said, "Aren't you going to take a look? What kind of man are you? What if it's a burglar?"

"Oh please, Carmen. I hear nothing, and you know I have to be up early tomorrow morn—"

Carmen squeezed his shoulder, this time with all her might, hoping all the inner turmoil rising within her would flood through him.

"Stop that," he said. "I'm going to sleep. You're overtired. But feel free to walk around the house in the middle of the night like a fool, for nothing."

"You can be a real asshole when you want, you know that?"

Michael didn't reply.

She reached to her side and turned on her bedside light, immediately comforted by the warm yellow light that illuminated her surroundings. A brief thought of grabbing her pillow to launch an assault on Michael passed.

Carmen listened. The tapping had ceased, but she remained unnerved. *I'll close the shower properly, just in case the sound comes back, and then he'll have to admit that he can hear it.* This plan of immediate action released some inner tension, as she put any thoughts of inspecting the ominous tapping sound that came down the passage on hold. It helped that the bathroom was on the opposite side of the room to the passage.

She climbed out of bed, slipped her feet into her faded pink slippers, and journeyed the few, yet labored steps to the bathroom. Reaching into the darkness, the hair on her outstretched right-arm stood up. She felt for the light switch against the bathroom's white tiled wall. Her breaths became audible.

Carmen tried to flick the light-switch on as soon as she felt it, in one efficient hand movement, but failed in connecting cleanly, and thus, failed to apply the required amount of force to fulfill her goal. *Damn it, damn it*, she thought, moving her hand back to the switch. This time she focused and felt the switch beneath her fingers.

She pressed down.

White light flooded the bathroom. Carmen's eyes shifted around the barren white-tiled walls, bearing a large mirror and medicine cabinet, with rapid quick-fire movements. She glanced over at the shower, toilet, and the bathroom countertop covered by an assortment of products. She exhaled, as her brain processed the expected images of her surroundings. She crossed the threshold into the bathroom with a step of confidence and walked a straight-line to the shower.

Carmen opened the shower's glass door, placing one foot inside. She shook her head as she watched a drop of water form on the showerhead. Gravity pulled the drop into a freefall until it hit the powder blue tiled shower floor—just missing her pink slipper. She turned the shower handle, closing it tight. Another drop of water hit her hand, the frigid drop heightening her senses, and a chill fled down her spine. She sensed something behind her—an urge to turn around enveloped her. *You're being silly*, her mind told her, *there's nothing*.

She tapped her foot on the shower's floor, as she waited to confirm the dripping had ceased. No more drops formed. Nodding to herself, she turned around, forcing herself to turn with the same speed as normal.

There was nothing behind her.

Halfway through the bathroom, she stopped mid-step. Something had set off a warning in her mind.

She put her foot down and turned to face the large mirror above the bathroom counter. There was an unexplainable feeling of irregularity in the mirror's world. She focused and tried to figure out what seemed off.

Nothing presented itself, and instead, Carmen noticed her ruffled, dark brown, shoulder-length hair and then her emerald green eyes, which looked tired. *Maybe I do need some rest*, she thought. *Maybe Michael was right, I am overtired and thus mistaken about the tapping I heard. The mind can play tricks on you when you're tired.* A weight lifted from her shoulders and procedural thoughts surfaced. She frowned at her appearance, her skin paler than she could recall, and then there was the frumpy white t-shirt and the black sweatpants she wore. Though disappointed, the new issues began to replace the fears from earlier, a trade she was more than happy to make.

She took a step closer to the mirror, even managing to smile at the idea of wearing something provocative tomorrow night to surprise Michael. The thoughts of what would ensue the following evening helped break the remaining shackles of the earlier fears. Feeling the best she had felt all-night, she ran the cold tap in the washbasin below the mirror, splashed some of its cool water over her face, and looked up.

She saw the words, "Help Me," scrawled over the center of the mirror, as if someone had blown breath and written with a finger. Carmen's eyes widened. She blinked. The words remained. The chill returned, shooting down her spine, and her heart began to pound inside her chest with renewed vigor.

Clarity hit.

Michael, you bastard, she thought.

She was about to turn and go curse her husband for playing such childish tricks on her, when a black cloak-like shadow flapped behind her. It was brief, but awoke primal instincts— fight or flight. The feeling of someone behind her resurfaced, she looked to the right of her reflection in the mirror.

"Michael! Michael! Help me!" Carmen screamed.

The flickering image of a pale-skinned, curly blonde-haired woman, dressed in a white bathrobe, reaching out with her hand, shook Carmen to the core. It took a split-second for the adrenaline to course through her veins. *Run*, her brain thundered. Before her next thought had time to form, she bolted out of the bathroom.

She fell over the bed in her haste to reach Michael, who jerked straight up, his startled eyes staring at his wife.

"What? What is it?" he said, reaching over to switch on his bedside light, which added to Carmen's light.

"There's someone . . . in the bathroom," Carmen said. Her face drained as her body shook.

"The bedroom's bathroom?"

"Yes."

Michael nodded. Carmen felt a sense of hope envelop her, knowing the expression on his face to be serious.

"Stay here," he said.

She nodded and gripped the maroon comforter tight.

Michael walked toward the bathroom.

The next moment he was inside.

Carmen's heart thundered within her chest, reverberating in her head.

The seconds ticked on in her mind. She braced through a shudder as she awaited Michael's reassurance. She couldn't handle the suspense.

She said, "Michael. Are you there?"

"I don't see anything," Michael said from within the bathroom.

"What?"

"There's no one here."

Carmen released her grip on the comforter and moved off the bed. She stood up and walked toward the bathroom.

Michael passed her as she was about to enter the bathroom. "Please, Carmen. I need to get some sleep."

She didn't reply. She looked at the doorway leading into the bathroom and held her breath, realizing she would need to cross the threshold again. She steadied herself, blocking the image of her last trip to the bathroom.

She entered.

There was no strange presence. She walked up to the mirror. *There's no writing*, she thought, staring at her reflection. She pushed through her heavy breathing and waited for something to happen, but nothing did. After a minute or two, her breathing found equilibrium. *No woman, nothing out of the ordinary. I must have imagined it, yeah, that's it*, she thought. *It was such a quick glimpse, and I've heard of people who imagine things when overtired. Yeah, it's definitely a symptom from lack of sleep. Now that I think about it, I can barely even recall how she looked.*

Carmen left the bathroom and took a seat on her side of the bed. Michael was asleep, facing the opposite wall. She reached toward her bedside light-switch and paused, holding close the comfort the light brought. After telling herself this was not the behavior of a grown woman, she reached further and gripped the switch.

Tap . . . tap . . . tap, tap, tap.

Her body froze, as if it had plunged into Arctic waters. *No, not the tapping again.* She contemplated waking Michael, but his earlier cold demeanor stopped her. *Fuck this. I'll check what's going on*, she thought. Having endured enough of the cat-and-mouse game with her fears, she willed herself calm and once more relegated the thoughts of impending doom to her overtired mind. *I'll go check and it'll be something stupid, then I can finally sleep.*

Carmen made her way to the stairway, regretting not taking up the electrician's offer of installing lights there when they had first bought the home. Instead, they had opted for the bare minimum when it came to repairs and new installations. That was over three months ago and the parsimoniousness had led her to the current predicament, requiring the dim light her cellphone provided to traverse through the darkness of the narrow passageway.

Having exited the bedroom, Carmen would not have to wait long to find the light she coveted. A faint light was flickering ahead of her against the wall on her left. Her pace toward the light, slow at first, quickened as she realized what it was.

She entered the living room, from where the light source came, shaking her head. She didn't even bother to switch on the room's light. *Damn it, Michael. You left the television on again*, she thought, exhaling out her mouth. A wave of relief washed over her, as she realized the TV had been the source of the strange noises. The woman she had seen in the bathroom must have been nothing more than the effects of an overtired mind.

Carmen smiled, wanting to laugh at herself.

She walked over to the coffee table, picked up the black remote, and turned to face the TV. Some war documentary in black and white filled the screen. She changed the channel, an instinctive reflex.

"So you believe we have to reach a different state of awareness to receive these thoughts?" the blonde woman on the screen said, wearing a charcoal power suit.

"Yes," said the old gray haired man in a neat, navy blue suit. "I believe when our senses are heightened, especially in extreme circumstances, we send out these waves. However, for the receiver to be able to intercept, interpret, and process them, they must be in a different state than our regular consciousness. I believe the key aspects to be the heightened state of the sender, and the altered state of the receiver, for this to work."

The man coughed. "Excuse me . . . These aspects are either pushing the limits of normal conscious thought, or not being shackled by it. For instance, I have studied some people who while dreaming in bed, or even sleepwalking, later claimed to be witnessing events unrelated to them. I've even looked into people having déjà vu when meeting a person for the first time. These events are all possible cases.'

A caption with his name appeared on the bottom of the screen. It read, "Professor Heinrich Stein-Wolff."

Professor Stein-Wolff continued. "Imagine one is in a great

state of either ecstasy or fear and then broadcasts these thoughts to the universe as brain waves. Some liken it to a form of telepathy, the transference of these images, sounds, or smells and even—"

Carmen pressed the off button. *What a load of shit*, she thought. *This is nonsense for people who should be asleep but end up watching instead.* Covered in darkness, she used the light from the cellphone to guide her back to the room. She shook her head as she thought about the night's adventure. *How silly I've been*, she thought.

She entered the stairway. Her warm and comfortable bed called for her.

Tap . . . tap . . . tap, tap, tap.

Carmen gasped, and a grunt-like sound escaped from her throat as the extra air came rushing in. Her arm jolted as she shined the light from the cellphone toward the noise. A noise, she knew, was coming from right in front of her.

At first, her brain refused to believe the information it received from her eyes, but as she held her gaze, the horror remained.

There was a balding man, dressed in a neat suit, hanging with a rope around his neck, right in the center of the stairway, barely two steps from her. His neat brown work-shoes dangled above the floor, and she watched as the right foot reached toward the floor.

Tap . . . tap . . . tap, tap, tap.

The sound of the right shoe tapping on the floor echoed in her head. She looked up, but the man's eyes were shut, his pallid face expressionless. As fast as the right foot had moved, it returned to hanging in the air, in unison with the left.

"Mi . . . Mi . . . Mi . . . chael," Carmen could barely talk, her words merely a whisper. She felt her body beginning to freeze, from the extremities in, as shock took control. Her legs weakened, and she had to lean against the wall of the stairway to keep her balance. She fought back. Adrenaline pumped and with it, her strength returned.

She bolted for the bedroom, screaming.

"Carmen, wake up!" She felt someone shaking her shoulder. "Carmen?"

Carmen realized it was Michael, and he was still shaking her as she opened her eyes, her body drenched in sweat. "What . . . What happened?" she said.

"You were having a nightmare. You scared the shit out of me," Michael said, rubbing her shoulder.

Carmen looked around the room. All the lights were on. She exhaled and noticed the time on the alarm clock: 2:17 a.m.

"Man that must've been some nightmare. You screamed like crazy," said Michael, concern etched into his face.

"Yeah, it was," she said. She couldn't believe how real it had all felt.

The sounds of sirens neared. They rose in volume until they exploded past their bedroom. Michael made his way to the window to see. Carmen didn't move.

"Wonder what's happening?" he said. "Oh, there goes an ambulance and a police vehicle . . . and another police car. Come check this out."

"No."

Michael shrugged. "I'm going to check the local news for anything on all those cops."

Carmen could see the intrigue all over Michael's face. She didn't reply, instead, she pulled the comforter over her chest and buried her head into her pillow. She heard Michael exit the bedroom.

She couldn't get back to sleep. Fragmented images of the nightmare flashed repeatedly in her mind's eye. After nearly half an hour, she heard footsteps approaching, and she raised her head slightly—watching the doorway.

Michael stuck his head in. "Hey, you should come check this. It's all over the local news."

"What?"

"Some guy, not even two blocks from us, on Straub Street, strangled his wife in their bathroom. Neighbors heard her screams and phoned the cops, but they were too late and they found him hanging in the stairway. They say he was already dressed for work. Isn't that the oddest thing?" Michael said, shaking his head.

Carmen didn't respond.

Michael sighed. "Well, that's what they're speculating on the news."

Again, she kept still.

Michael walked over to her, took a seat on the bed alongside her, and began stroking her shoulder again. "I'm sorry, babe. Forget all that other shit. What was your nightmare about? Do you remember?"

149

Carmen looked at him with vacant eyes. The color on her face had drained and once more, she felt the grip of an ominous frigid chill. Horrifying images of her nightmare kept invading her thoughts. She tried to fight back. *It was just a bad dream, just a coincidence what Michael saw on the news*, she told herself.

"Well? You remember it?" Michael said.

She turned over, facing away from him, and said, "I don't remember it."

"Come on now, babe."

"I said I don't remember. Now leave me alone," she said. She shut her eyes. *Just a bad dream, just a coincidence.*

Carmen gripped the comforter tightly around herself.

Another variation of John D. Stanton's cover art.

Justin Hunter

Feel the Sun

There was a time when you walked the hallways of darkness and you danced. People passed by you and you would greet them. The journey was always from one end of the maze to the next. Upon reaching the end of the maze, you would promptly turn around and retrace your steps. The pathway of the maze was always the same. Same doors. Same paths. Same people.

There was hate in the people. Unrecognized at first. Not ignored, for they would follow you and ask you questions that never had a correct answer. They would pull at your body when you danced by them. They would greet you, you would greet them, and they knew you were the enemy. The people meant fear and it began to change you. You would learn to walk the ground directly in the center of the hallways. The dancing erodes from your soul. Your feet do not dance anymore. You greet the people with the same words, slamming your head up and down. It's not a greeting anymore, but an acknowledgement of fellowship. What kind of fellowship? It doesn't matter. What matters is sameness. There is safety there and you take it. You walked the pathway when it was dangerous and now you want to walk it in safety. Not because you want too, but just because you must. Every time you hit the end of the maze, you would have to turn abruptly around and stalk the corridors again. The people began to know you and they would wait for you.

They test you. They ask you questions. They hurt you with every answer you give.

They take your imagination and make it your enemy. Flight of fancy brings cuts. Imagination brings scars. To feel is to be harmed. So you don't feel anymore.

You tromp back and forth along the same lines. You grow small in person. You become like the others. Never the questioner – you are always the prey. You are stalked, always.

Sometimes you float. Your feet don't touch the ground. The others see you float and demand your feet touch the ground. Sometimes you can make them. Other times your feet betray you. You cannot touch the ground. You were never meant to walk the same walk as the others. Nobody can hide forever. They hurt you. You learn.

The routine seems endless. You become less sure. You begin to limp. Your spine curves like a shepherd's crook. Your head hangs at your breastbone. Your chin thumps against your chest, making your teeth chatter together. The people think you are talking, but it's only the clacking of bone upon bone. There is no flesh in your words.

The people don't let you float anymore. They've tugged you down to the floor. They sit on your back as you crawl the maze. Back and forth. Your flesh grinds into the ground. There is less and less of you with each passing. You crawl over bits of yourself. You slide in your down filth. The people don't laugh. They don't chide. They just are. They don't consume you. You are killing yourself just fine.

Just fine.

A new way out opens up in before you. Where it comes from doesn't matter. It's there.

You want to burn. You stomp toward an open courtyard of twisted metal in the hope of seeing the sun. To die in the light. You leave the corners and are out in the open and two beings of dust and flesh and rusted metal armor walk along the grounds. In one of their robot hands is a gun. The other is an open sore the shoots fire. The beings of dust shoot fire without warning or meaning. The courtyard burns and soon you will burn with it. Therefore, you go out in the open and duck back into the hallways so as not to be seen by the machines. You want to feel the sun. You don't want to burn where the shadows are the only things left dancing. When you scurry out into the open you can see the sun shining overhead, but you can't feel it. There is no warmth. Only fire.

You cannot hide from the machines forever and soon the machines see you and they call to you. You feel nothing. One of the two doesn't seem to care about you anymore and wanders off. It meanders and burns and you are less than nothing—but the other machine is very interested. It calls to you and you float toward the rafters on the outskirts of the courtyard. Your feet never leaving the ground when you're out in the open. The only way to fly is when you have a ceiling overhead. There is inherent safety in limitation. Creativity is death. Others will know and kill you.

The machine raises his gun hand and fires. The bullet goes past your face. You don't feel. You don't fear. You bob down and again the machine fires. It always misses. For it can't hit a non-person. It questions you but you don't hear the words. You feel the commands. It tells you that feet must not leave the ground for more than a moment when walking. Floating is dissention and you force yourself to sink. Then the ground is the enemy and you must float. You change and conform. Every order a lobotomy. Every knife through the synapse is a blessing.

The fire burns around you. The death machines vanish. The fire burns everything, but you feel no pain and you don't feel the sun. The colors of the fire dance on your body. They don't light up your surroundings. They're just another color that means nothing to you. It doesn't light up anything inside. Fire has no meaning. It doesn't burn. Anything without pain has no meaning.

You splay your arms toward the cloudy sky overhead. The limited universe is consumed by fire. There is nobody left to kill you. Nobody cares anymore what you do. There is just you and the sky. No smoke. Useless fire. Dead Sun.

There is no point is looking up anymore. You see, but there is nothing inside that registers. When there is nobody left to kill you then life has no meaning. Take in the grey. Take in the black. Take in the red, orange, and purple of the fire. Let the flesh leave your body. Let your bones be ground into dust. Let no stone stand upon another. Lost. Artless. Man grinds man to nothing. Not even the worms will eat the rancid flesh.

For it is tasteless.

Kyle Rader

Jump

Morning air through a barely cracked window often feels refreshing; as if the day is gently prodding you awake. The wind that Sydney felt was anything but. Cold and filled with dead leaves and flecks of dirt. Not prodding so much, rather rape brought her to consciousness.

Her head hurt. A lot. Her eyes refused to open and, when they did, a monstrous world awaited her. It spun and spun, the white ceiling turning into a carousel. The contents of her stomach found themselves upon her blouse. The stench curled into her nostrils and she spent several minutes dry heaving.

When the violence of her awakening passed, Sydney realized that she didn't know where she was. What was the last thing she did recall? Having dinner and a quick drink with the girls from the bank at Jerry's Pub then going home. *Wait,* she thought, *do you actually remember getting into the car? Do you remember going home?*

She was panicking, she knew. Probably for no good reason at all. She was sure there was a logical explanation to the entire situation, one that would cause her to have a good laugh once her head stopped impersonating a kettledrum.

Her hair fell into her eyes; the wind gushed in with another salvo. When she reached to brush it away, she discovered her arms bound by beige mechanical restraints attached to a chair, a dentist's chair it seemed.

Only her head could move with any kind of freedom.

Where the hell is the wind coming from? Pain from the bits of nature it regurgitated onto her face and opened several cuts.

No open window that brought the elements into her cell. An entire section of the wall was missing. Sydney thought of foxholes and bombings she'd seen online from war-torn regions. The black char around the epicenter and the crags of sheetrock protruding out of the building like teeth from a broken jaw, all of it, just like a war-zone. But, she was in no warzone. The message painted in white on the floor confirmed she was in a place far, far worse.

It said, in clear, block letters, *Jump.*

Eardrum splitting buzzing and she was free. Sydney tumbled from the chair; linoleum punched the breath from her lungs so she couldn't even whimper. She scuttled to the far corner of the room, away from the hole, away from the demand.

The sky in the world outside her cell was gray, overcast, and morose. Distant treetops of a forest appeared at floor-level. Sydney hobbled to the hole; her legs, deadened from atrophying rest. She had to. She had to see what lay beyond. She had to show she was not afraid.

A parking lot with tufts of weeds and grass piercing through the pavement formed into a cul-de-sac shape with what was once a topiary in the middle, resembling the eye of a giant corpse, lay below. Sydney clutched the side of the blown-out wall and leaned out, a gust of wind nearly knocking her free. By her count, she was ten floors up. *Ten floors,* she thought. *That's like one hundred feet!*

Sydney scanned the horizon, seeking signs of civilization. The building must be close to others. *Why would anyone construct a ten-story building in the middle of nowhere?* Trees upon trees upon trees. That's all there was. She slowly walked back from the hole, holding her breath. For on the ground below, the pavement was cracked, and stained red with blood.

Sydney lay on her back, staring at the popcorn ceiling. She'd explored her cell and confirmed the obvious: the hole in the wall was the only way out. A few empty cabinets mounted into the walls and the chair was all that occupied the space, save for her.

Escape seemed impossible, at least for the moment, at least physically. Sydney retreated into her mind, away from the sick game that someone was forcing her to play. She went back to the previous day. Work was routine. New loans, mortgage refinancing, the usual. She greeted customers with the kind of warmth that she would've expected if she were in their shoes. While other loan officers cared only for their numbers, Sydney genuinely cared for the people. She wanted to help them out, whether it was young couples starting out or those who were just trying to keep their heads above water. She laughed with them and she cried with them. In the three years she'd been at the bank, she'd become the customer's favorite.

A few of them went straight to Jerry's after work. Sydney changed from her work dress into a sweater and jeans, though this attempt to make herself plain did nothing of the sort. Sydney was striking. The kind of natural good looks that people, men and women, could not help but admire. Some felt she was stuck up, just another hot chick with the perfect body who used it to get ahead. This was before they spoke to her and realized this was far from the truth. She was a genuine nice person. Some called her a saint, though she laughed this off.

Why, then, would someone do this to her? To her, someone who'd never said a bad word about anyone, who saw the good in everyone and would break her back to help anyone if she could? *It doesn't make sense,* Sydney thought. *None of this makes any sense.*

Sydney went through the evening as much as she could remember. She'd two drinks and chicken parmesan for dinner. Three men asked her for her number and she politely turned them down. Her head was clear when she left her friends. Her little Kia was fifteen feet from the door in a brightly lit parking lot. *Why can't I remember getting into it?*

Frustration had her fists meeting the walls. She beat the sheetrock until her knuckles split and imprints of red ran down to the floor in tandem with the day's sun. A handful of streetlights, specters cursed to haunt the parking lot, came alive. They provided no comfort, for the faint light reflected into the room, causing the white letters of the taunt to glow and chase her into her dreams.

The messages multiplied while Sydney slept, growing from one to four. Painted in haste, the letters were runny, the paint still drying. Each said the same word: Jump. *The cowards,* she thought, *of course they'd come in while I was asleep.* The thought should've frightened her, that her captor had such ease of access to her and could, in theory, slink right in and toss her out to her death with her being none the wiser. Yet, it exhilarated her, for it meant that there was another way out of the room other than suicide.

Sydney spent the better part of the day knocking against the walls and listening for hollow points. She picked at the edges of the linoleum tiles until every fingernail broke. Exhausted, she collapsed against the dentist's chair, soaked in sweat, sweat that became a shroud of ice with the winds from outside.

Has to be a way, she thought. *Has to be.*

By this time, Sydney was thirsty. No available water source led her resorting to licking the beads of sweat from her arms. Aside from a momentary dampness, her tongue remained swollen; her throat cracked. She had to escape, and fast. She remembered hearing that you could last only a few days without water. She was pushing two. If she couldn't find her tormentor's secret passageway, she would grow far too weak to resist should he (at she assumed it was a he) grow weary of the game.

The only object remaining for observation was the chair itself. The mechanical restraints looked like claws ready to crush her. It was bolted to the floor and could be raised and lowered by way of a manual hydraulic foot lever. She raised it as high as it could go, and then sent it back down. It hissed as the pressure released, yet no passage lay revealed.

"Goddamnit! Goddamnit!" Sydney picked at the bolts affixed to the floor before giving up and curling up next to the chair, her head clogged with mucus, and her eyes irritated from drying tears.

Snuffing out the glowing words of suggestion, the night engulfed the fuzzy streetlamps. Heavy clouds were the culprit. They surged over the top of the trees, making straight for the building, for Sydney. To take her mind off the freezing, Stygian nightmare, she again wandered through the previous night. She could see her Kia in the parking lot. She remembered squinting from the reflection of some passing headlights in her driver side window. *I turned back toward the bar then,* she thought. *I saw Janey and Thom laughing at something. Thom was eating a mozzarella stick and the cheese kept going out further and further. Yeah, that's right.*

"Why can't I remember anything else?" she whispered as the rain arrived. It started as a drizzle but escalated into a downpour. Her mouth lusting for water, Sydney crawled to the hole, sticking a cupped hand out. Even with the frequency of the rain, she only managed to get less than a thimbleful. Still, she slurped and slurped, growing more frustrated with every handful, as if nature itself fought against her.

Stubbornness kept her at it long into the evening. Only when her shoulders refused to move her arms anymore did Sydney quit. She was thirsty, but a bit less so. She lay on her back, letting her head stick out of the hole so the rain could wash away the grime and sweat. Laughing, she hollered into the storm, hoping that who or whomever had put her here was listening. "I'm not going to die here. No matter what, I'm never jumping."

Sydney fell asleep with a smirk upon her face. Her little victory proved a powerful sedative.

More taunts presented themselves in her cell upon her waking, this time, in multiple colors and styles. Cursive, block and even spray-painted expanded from the area around the hole and into the room. Sydney held back a scream with her hands when she saw her captors had outlined her entire body in 'Jump's.

The fear did not last. Anger, a pure hate, had her screaming obscenities at the walls and ceiling. "Come and face me, you sons-of-bitches! I'm just a tiny girl. What are you afraid of, huh?

"You can put as many signs up as you want. Carve them into the floor for all I care. I'm not going to do it. Never!" Sydney leaned out of the hole, grabbing the sides and swaying back and forth, as she used to as a kid playing on the jungle gym. More defiance. Pointless, perhaps, but she knew that it would get their attention.

"Yes, you will." Sydney's fingers slipped as she rocked forward, leaving her wobbling on the precipice, her own momentum acting as Judas. "No, no, no," she leaned back as far as she could, waving her arms in circles. The horizon came at her, angling sharply down as she moved closer to the Jump. She stuck her rear out and bent at her knees. It was crude, but it was enough to shift her weight and deposit her on the floor.

"Nice recovery."

"Show yourself, you scumbag!" Sydney growled the last insult, trying to sound more intimidating than she felt. In reality, her brush with death had her shaken up. If the owner of the voice walked in at that very moment, she would more than likely burst into hysterics.

"Sorry. I'm a visitor here, just like you."

The voice came from the other side of the wall, the one closest to the hole. How had she not heard anyone over there before? The wind? The storm? *On the other hand, maybe the guy didn't feel much like conversing,* Sydney thought. "What's your name?"

"Geoffrey."

"I'm Sydney, Geoffrey. It's nice to meet you." The words, so long engrained into her as the right and proper thing to say, seemed now downright vulgar. Geoffrey felt this way as well, evidenced by a long sigh. Still, Sydney was glad to meet another person, especially one in the same predicament. It gave her hope, something she was quickly running short on. "What do you mean 'visitor'?"

"Oh, that we are both just passing through this place."

"And where is 'this place'? Do you know? Do you know how we got here? Who is doing this to us?"

"Come to the hole."

The face she saw poking over the threshold was not at all what she expected. In her mind, Geoffrey was young, still with some life left inside of him, like her. A ghoul greeted her instead. The rings under his eyes were deep enough she could see his bony eye sockets. His cheeks were gaunt, his lips, corpse-white and cracked. "This place is just that, a place. We are in many of them in our lives. This one happens to be our last." He spoke with a smirk, and it, along with a joyful sheen in his eyes, hinted at a complete mental break.

"How long have you been here?" Sydney edged away from Geoffrey. He would have to stretch far, but she was still close enough for him to grab hold of her.

"Longer than most, shorter than some."

"I can't remember how I got here, can you?"

"Does it matter? We're here."

"Yes, it goddamn matters! Someone took us away from our lives! I want to know who and why we are here!"

Geoffrey grinned. The gauntness of his face accentuated his skeletal features. "Ah, now you are asking the right question. How we got here and who put us here? That's irrelevant. However, the *why?* Now, there's something to be explored.

"They can see us. You know that. Right? The new words they write while we sleep?"

Sydney nodded. "They're taunting us. Trying to break our nerves."

"Taunting? You poor woman, they are encouraging us."

Sydney turned away from her neighbor in disgust. She hugged herself, rubbing her arms in a vain attempt to warm herself. *Encouraging us? This guy is nuts. Why would anyone encourage someone into suicide?* Feeling his eyes still upon her, she turned back. "We're being punished, aren't we?"

"Don't be naïve. Punishment is not the goal here. If it were, we'd be stuck out on planks without much of a choice. That's the key: choice. Here we are given the choice on how to escape."

Tears were in her eyes and on her face. Sydney didn't even realize it, though Geoffrey did and for a moment, his insanity softened. "Oh, don't cry, Sydney. Don't do that. This isn't a sad thing. It's joyous! Soon, you'll be free from the shackles that bind us here."

"I like my life. I-I just want to go home."

Geoffrey put a finger to his lips. "And so you shall, dear Sydney. You'll see it soon."

With that, he let go of the wall and jumped.

Sydney watched him the entire way down, despite the voice in her head telling her to look away. Geoffrey made no sound at all, his arms outstretched, Christ-like. What frightened Sydney the most was his face. As it dropped, faster and faster, it seemed to increase in serenity. By the time he reached the ground, he was smiling.

The impact removed this in a flash. His mouth opened as his skull broke apart. His poor, demented mind exited like foam from a shaken up beer car. As his blood became just another stain on the pavement, three strangers emerged from the ground floor. They were clad in hazmat suits and gasmasks. A body bag was placed next to Geoffrey's remains. Two of the strangers shoved him inside while the third scooped up his brains in a large Tupperware container. They were on their way inside when Sydney yelled to them.

"You sick bastards! I'm never jumping, you hear me? You'll have to throw my starved, dead body out of here. Do you understand? *I'm not jumping!*"

The stranger with the container of grey matter paused as the others re-entered the building. The stranger regarded Sydney as if she were some kind of curiosity in a sideshow. Then, the stranger waved to her. It was not vitriolic, nor taunting. The stranger behaved as if Sydney was an old friend, like one spotted from across the street.

Sydney spat; the wind carried it far away. She managed to tear one of the dusty cabinets free from the wall. Lifting it over her head, she brought it down against the floor repeatedly until it was nothing but splintered pieces of particleboard. She held the largest piece up and circled the room as to demonstrate to the unseen cameras just how much fight remained within her.

Exhausted, she sat in a corner and wandered off inside her memories for a time until a scream from outside, followed by a thud shocked her into reality.

Sydney didn't bother to look this time.

When the night reached its apex of darkness, the wall of Sydney's cell pushed inward. The hidden door, one she sought for, opened just wide enough for a person to step through. A faceless person crept into the room like a golem, the stature and the jutting tents through the front of the hazmat suit revealed the stranger to be a woman. On her belt was a small canister. Gas, a small amount of a very powerful kind designed for one purpose: to put people into a dreamless unconsciousness. This was how they took Sydney and the others. It was how they kept them docile at night, so they could enter undetected and paint more signs.

This stranger had been attending to Sydney since they brought her to her cell. She took a special relish in the young woman, as she showed an inordinate amount of willpower. Much more so than the previous occupants. Still, they anticipated her reserves of defiance to be exhausted soon and out she'd go.

Nevertheless, there was work to do, so she went to give Sydney a dose of her medicine, but she stepped in something wet as she approached. Upon the stranger's head lay a pair of night vision goggles, specially made to fit over the gasmask. Turning them on, the world glowed in a blinding green, before it settled into a visible pattern, revealing the wet, slippery substance to be blood.

There was a lot of it; the source of origin was Sydney, who lay face down, curled into the fetal position. The mystery guest panicked, pacing around the cell. A small walkie-talkie switched on with a hiss. As she raised it to report the suicide, a violent push came from behind, sending her straight out of the hole and the cold ground below.

Sydney was in the barely lit hallway before the faceless woman hit the ground, pausing to rip her shirt off and wrap a poor-man's tourniquet around the inside of her elbow, where she'd taken a sizeable chunk out of herself. She hoped that she'd not lost so much blood that she'd pass out during her escape.

The hall resembled that of a hotel; rooms closely next to each other with the "doors" controlled by contraptions one would expect to see in bank vaults. Sydney knew that there were others trapped within, others suffering. *Nothing I can do about that. Not now. Get out and get help.*

Finding the stairwell at the end of the hall, Sydney moved fast, so fast she lost her footing and ended up sliding down to floor nine. The door to each floor was locked with some kind of keycard system newer than the building itself. She thought *not important, get to the ground floor.* She ignored the nagging pessimistic thought that it too would be locked in the same way.

By divine providence, or dumb luck, it was not. Sydney almost laughed in relief, but an alarm jarred her. They knew she was out. They would know she'd be coming here, looking to leave in a fashion that was not deadly to her. Footsteps rushing toward her confirmed this. She couldn't go back up; they'd see her and toss her back in that room, probably right out of the window for the murder she'd committed. What then? Fight them? Push through and take her chances?

As the handle of the door pushed down, Sydney flattened herself against the wall in the corner where the door swung open. It bounced off her, not enough for anyone to think a person was hiding behind it. She bit her lip as many yellow-booted people that ran past her. She waited until the last disappeared and slid out of her hiding place and through the door as it closed.

The room was a large lobby, devoid of nearly any furniture. Large frosted glass doors led outside, to what she hoped was her salvation. Two of her captors stood between her and freedom. Two captors with very large guns.

Sydney ran in a crouch to a main desk, the only relic left from the time the building served a purpose other than cruelty. She crawled underneath the desk, hugging her knees to her chest, holding her breath. She sat there, looking around at her now limited surroundings. If she couldn't get out the front, she'd have to go out the back. *There has to be a back entrance or a fire exit, doesn't there?* She dared to lean forward for a glance; her eyes scanned the area for a single heartbeat.

The familiar red glow of an Exit sign was close enough for her to touch. Sydney didn't waste any time. She ran low to the ground as if she was running in a cave, not looking to the front door, for she knew if she did, she would freeze. *Just go,* she kept thinking. The mantra kept her from wondering what the bullets would feel like as they shredded her apart.

This did not happen. She opened the door, holding the handle and releasing it in millimeter increments to prevent a metallic click. She expected another door leading to freedom. Instead, she found herself in the hollowed out remains of a hall, the sheetrock hammered away, allowing access to an adjoining office. A blue glow reflected in her eyes, calling to her. Sydney knew that she must keep moving, but the office promised answers, she just knew it. She had to know why she'd been subjected to such inhuman treatment; *had to.*

Flat-screen monitors, rows upon rows of them were mounted on the wall. Each looked into a different cell, at another prisoner. Some of them raged against their predicament, like Sydney. Others despaired. A few of the cells were empty, like hers.

Upon the adjacent wall lay pictures, hundreds of pictures of each person taken along with documents and notes of each. Sydney ran her fingers over them, in haste, ripping many from their thumbtacks. She found Geoffrey. His section showed him smiling with children, in hospitals and doing other charity. There was no trace of the broken mind she saw at the end of his life. Her eyes were drawn to a number. It was scrawled in marker on a piece of white tape in what was clearly an unsteady hand. 6, it read. Nothing further. No explanation, no big reveal. Just a number.

Sydney found her own face, which covered an entire section. Images of her from high school, college, work, all showing her smiling, laughing, and enjoying life. "Oh god," she said as she saw a picture of her at Jerry's.

She too, had a number, save for hers came with a warning: *10. Highly infectious. Anyone exposed to this vector must report the following symptoms immediately: Excessive smiling, uncommon laughter, elation, a desire to make others feel joy. Failure to do so will result in neutralization.*

Everyone on the board had a number assigned, between one and ten. Above the picture wall, was a lone message, it too, spray-painted in white letters. It read, "Happiness is contagious."

She backed from the wall of joy and bumped into the wall of monitors, which swayed precariously. Sydney rushed to steady them as the plastic creaked against the metal brackets affixing them to the wall. In the process, her palm smashed down upon a keyboard. The screens switched from the room feeds to a video. A man seated at a desk appeared, flanked by two others, both wearing hazmat suits.

"This facility is the first of many in what will be a global effort. In the first quarter alone, we've identified and neutralized forty vectors, none lower than a six on the contagion scale, with three tens eliminated in the past two weeks alone. Our preliminary estimates show that this will reduce the infection rate within the local population by eleven percent—"

"I infect people because I'm happy? Th—that doesn't make sense!"

"---*Happiness is a cancer. It is a contagion, spreading false hope and ultimately, discontent to the world. This falsity makes us complacent, unaware of the true nature of the world. We are ill prepared for catastrophe, war, famine. Happiness is the precursor to our extinction.*

"*Drastic measures must be taken, and ARE being taken, to stamp out the vectors. We cannot simply remove them from the board. We must rehabilitate them, CURE them, else their corpses will remain able to spread the contagion. We need to make them feel the disease devouring them. Then, and only then, can we help them. One by one, we shall burn them out of our world and re-write it anew, free for the pure. It may take decades, but we will succeed. We have to. For our grandchildren.*"

Rubber gloves held Sydney close. A needle penetrated her taught neck, sending her into a nothingness.

Wind licked her back into the world once again, stronger than before, cutting her down to her marrow. Blinking away the murk, Sydney wished she'd remained in her forced slumber.

She lay upon a wooden plank outside of the building. There were no handholds and it wobbled as she shifted her weight. Splinters drove into her arms and hands as she hugged it for a fleeting sense of security. Was this punishment for the woman she'd killed? *No, this is revenge,* she thought, biting her lip to stop her from crying. That satisfaction she would *not* give them.

An air horn blasted her ears; the echo vanished into the distant forest. It repeated itself and the plank began to move backward. "Oh, God." Sydney turned on her hip, only to suffer a final taunt. The hole with the wall it was born from, with a slit at the bottom just big enough for the plank. One last message greeted her, a final thought to ponder; *you should have jumped.*

"I told you I would never jump and I won't!" Sydney stood on the rickety plank, her final defiance. Inches from the wall, she banged her palms against it. "I beat you. *I beat you all!*"

The plank vanished into the building. Sydney dropped to the waiting parking lot, laughing, not out of spite, but of joy.

Third variation of John D. Stanton's cover art.

Alex S. Johnson

Numinoids

I. Prolegomena to any future Metaphysics of the Numinoids

They had never been seen before, in the same way that they've always been seen.

Numinoids twisted categories, flailed logic, presented a blank and nebulous target.

Tensions rippled across the political spectrum; spectral fingers probed and tested fault lines. The frailty of the New Order was revealed as never before. Virtual drill bits of a Newer Order spat curled shavings of code as they drilled, baby, drilled, down to foundations cloaked in the mummified hides of Cromwell's Jesters, late of Strawberry Hill.

There were calls for "more grotesques" and "fewer divisions" between "heaven and earth," "sky and water," "machines and gods."

Yet the vast majority of citizens went about their business as usual. They had no opinions. They had food, and clothing, and housing, and employment, and entertainment, bar snacks and tinctures of opium, Meta-reality shows, android slaves, and a ceaseless stream of clown porn.

Those with the right eyes had never not seen the Numinoids; their invisible handiwork was everywhere.

In Buckingham Palace, Cyber Regina resumed her old regimen of cannabis oil, and her ratings soared briefly, as she extolled the health benefits of "a good puff on a gray day." The Prime Minister jacked himself into the portals of a cosmic-orgasmic egg, and sheet lightning flashed through the offices on Downing Street, revealing ecstatic skeletons that danced like early black and white cartoons.

In Parliament, Guy Fawkes was hailed as "the man with the monster plan" and in place of effigies stuffed with firecrackers, a real-time, living installation allowed visitors to walk around inside his brain, slip-slide along neural connections and catch the scrolling tails of comedies sparked by the improvised patter of Synaptic Gore Minstrels.

But these were effects of the Numinoidal invasion, and rarely, if ever, attributed to the cause. The cause was not understood. The cause had no face, no program. It was humanity's reaction to the metamachinegods that shaped them, cast them into tangible forms. Made them objects of an unknown worship. Fractured society's spine. Infused politics with a tonic of gaiety and license.

As They watched, and learned, and jotted down notes.

II. Spyworld V. Numinoids

The British special services had gone on high alert. Borders between worlds had melted once more, or were on the verge; metallic droplets splattered down a recursive spiral. When protease cookie cutters snapped the bolts, London Bridge wouldn't just fall—it would freeze, a pixelated smear suspending passenger's mid-journey. Not that this was the work of the Numinoids, exactly; the jury was also hung in quantum space, waiting for one precise shot from the pistol that usually decided these matters.

Down in the quarry dug from the Archbishop of Canterbury's enormous bollocks, clerks worked around the clock re-digitizing the data in the hope it would deliver different results; but the pistol was missing, presumed lodged in the inner lining of Canterbury's scrotal sac, and a looping effect had, or was rumored to have, taken hold.

Tissue samples of those infected with numinosity taken at the scene of impossible crimes had been delivered across oceans of time to arrive at a foreordained impasse. It was extraordinarily difficult to distinguish between the forensic detectives, their methodology, and the evidence itself. The hourglass was running away, pumping legs of sodden sand, and Downing Street demanded immediate results. As the Prime Minister himself put it, in a rare appearance outside the egg-womb, "these Nano-aggressions will not stand." He did not attribute this novel form of terrorism to the Numinoids, but to unnamed and unnamable forces of subversion.

WRINKLE TO: Thames House, where sloppy organisms derived from black, distorted masses of detective/methodology/evidence passed from hand to vinyl-gloved hand, coordinated with split-second timing. One false move and the tenuous bonds that held MI-666 together would snap, plunging London into several variorum folios of a new Dark Age.

Kensington Brothers, the Earl of Nowhere Man, strode into the War Room. He wore a micropore buttocksclencher over a demi-business dress of chopped liver. Half his face trailed off down mirrored corridors; he reached up and snatched the elastic strands, reeling in his visage minus an eyeball crunched through a data compiler, and spewed out to waiting journalists outside the flesh-cordon blocking off Lambeth Bridge. Whereupon Brothers' vision split up and morphed into spidery machines, with the usual awkward sequel.

"Well fuck my face off!" said Brothers. The agents snapped to attention and plopped the organisms into a trough that crawled away into the bowels of esoteric formulae. When their boss's mug was fully retrieved, it had bloomed to *profondo rosso* with just a hint of boiled lobster. "Nobody leaves this room until I find out who leaked the file on the Numinoids."

"But we *are* the Numinoids," said Mimsy Borogrove, an Indonesian agent recruited from a dungeon stuffed for storage in Westminster Abbey and recently rediscovered fused with poet Aphra Behn's bones. "We are the change, the hope, the expectation..."

"Oh spare me the Creed," barked Brothers as the others began to mouth the Numinous Litany. "These things are *not* our friends. How many times do I have to tell you, they're invaders from another dimension, hell-bent on gene tweaking the human race for sheer sport? Bloody hell, the whole lot of you is contaminated, converts to an obscenity, obsequious goons bowing before an altar of ichor. Et cetera, et cetera, et cetera."

He sank to his seat and scooted toward the steel desk, piled high with papers, transcripts, and psych tests and the Revelations of Akkan-Li, which went to 1,000 pages of triple-encrypted hard copy. Brushing his fingers across his chrome-plated dome, he discovered a few Numinoidrones that had dug themselves into the metal sheeting. "Hold still, you beasts." Their screams echoed down the halls of Thames House.

"This is the Prime Minister," came a voice from sound-sculpting cones embedded in the ceiling's acoustic reptile. "What in the actual fuck is going on down there? I think I've made it blindingly clear that this government does not condone on-site torture porn. It's all over the Intrawebs. Several dozen flashmobs have already gathered in Hyde Park and Kensington Gardens, awaiting instructions from...*Them.*"

Brothers dangled two Numinoids between his thumb and forefinger, and then set them gently down in a jar of glowing vapor. "Patch these fellows into the mainframe," he growled. "I want to know what they know that we think we know."

"Don't you think we should listen to the Prime Minister?" squeaked Borogrove. "If we don't have his support, we might as well say goodbye to MI-666 entirely. He *likes* them. On the other hand, we might be able to learn something from our handlers..."

"*What* did you call them?"

"Sorry," said Borogrove, flicking a nanodrone cluster from the collar of her box-suit. "I just meant that extreme interrogation is a thing of the past, don't you agree? Even if, technically, the mainframe's programming is responsible."

"Your penchant for rhetorical questions annoys me," said Brothers. "I'm of a mind to have you transferred back to storage." He rose and faced the agents, who had retreated, backs against the wall, fearing their boss's wrath.

"To borrow a line from St. Nixon, I would like to make one thing perfectly clear. We are still an agency of Her Cybermajesty's government. We are not here to retroengineer the wheel. We are also not here to clean up any terroristic messes. Like my mother, I have a downright horror of the 'eyeball in the soup' trope that's been circulating heavily in recent days. Once the peepers have splashed down in the minestrone, it's a spectacular waste of labor trying to push them back into their gory sockets. By which I mean, via an extended metaphor..."

But the agents were completely bewildered. He wondered if his nightly tonic, a cocktail of the Dream Liquid and Essence of Georges Bataille, had begun to dissolve his judgment.

"I am not stepping down from my post!" he blurted out suddenly.

"Nobody said anything about a step-down, Sir. That's not a call anybody here can make. But I think I understand what you're on about." This from Squires Mobley, who'd been with the department for so long that no one remembered how he'd gotten there in the first place. Squires was an Indeterminate, a new breed of human quantum-breed and subject to the eye of the beholder. When Brothers looked at him directly, Squires resembled a sort of melon on stilts.

"Please elaborate," said Brothers, sinking to the floor, his head in his hands. "I would love to hear this." He had persistent surreal nightmares about melons on stilts, flashbacks from the Tar on Werror.

"What I believe you're saying is..." Squires reformatted. "Sorry. I think you're getting at a fundamental dilemma in our democracy. We're caught between the Scylla of putrid gentech and the Charybdis of the New Church of Noumen. The citizens are confused; and, to be frank, so are many government workers. Yes, democracy is messy, and sometimes brutal games become necessary to disinter the Starbaby from the pyramid's eye, so to speak..."

"Get to the bloody point, man!" shouted Brothers. "I have such a migraine right now, and I don't have time for your jargon. I wish I'd never heard of the Numinoids. Drill down, they said, down through the politically correct suicide vests, to the epistemological core, the meat of the matter. And all of you marched like lemmings to their tune. Marched like..."

Borogrove rushed to Brothers with a handful of purple capsules and a paper cup. "You're over-wrought, boss. I think we all are. Even I, who have been inducted into the NCN and serve as Priestess—have doubts. Where is this all leading? Will reality, as we know it, simply collapse into a black hole, turning civilization itself a clot of bollocks-scrape? So much depends on getting that pistol back online. Never mind a red wheelbarrow, glazed with rain water..."

"I agree 100%," said Brothers, tossing down the pills and gulping the water in the cup. "We'll defer grilling the interlopers until we excavate the Reality-Hacked Glock 17 Gen4. Can someone get me a visual on the Archbishop's nuts?"

"Right away, sir," said Squires. His fingers blurred as they danced over the keyboard grown from his stomach, and the wraparound wall screen scrolled out a graphic.

"Eww," said Borogrove.

"I know, right?" said Brothers. "It looks like tapioca balls floating in some kind of pink...jelly. Where's the Glock?"

"We'll have to delimit the pistol from its mythical parameters," said Squires, breathing heavily. "It's sunk in patriarchal logic like a fly in amber. If we aren't extremely careful, we risk losing the plot entirely. The tissue is wedded to the Glock's outer membrane. Sticky work. Delicate.

"All right," he added, patting his forehead with a green felt pad, "I think we're getting somewhere now. Could somebody lend me a spanner?"

Sonrise tossed him the tool. Squires gripped his bellydrive's main bolt and twisted once, twice, three times, until Lady Luck showed him his fortune, trivialized for her pleasure. "Almost there," he grunted. "Now...this building is either going to explode in 30 seconds, incinerting all personnel, or we'll finally be able to see the gun's corona."

At which point, the spidery machines built from wedges of Brothers' former eye jumped the barrier and began to crawl up the walls of Thames House.

III. Stigmata Martyr

Things like golden fish slipped through her hands as the rain poured steadily, monotonously. All the good was pouring down the drain; Robin Sobbs could follow it with her eyes, but paralysis had otherwise set in. That, and her face felt borrowed.

The cathedrals walked through the city, chanting hymns to death. Their stained glass mouths opened like charnel houses crammed with slimy bones, as the storm continued to pound the pavements, and the fishlike beings fell through the holes in Robin's new stigmata. Martyrdom was a fashion taking hold of everyone she knew, except for members of her immediate family, who still scoffed at the coming of the Numinoids.

Robin opened the yellow umbrella and, looking both ways, crossed the thoroughfare, stepping carefully over dank, sour-smelling puddles. The cathedrals reflected in the water looked like dark, hunched dwarves. She made her way to the top of the stairs leading down into the flat she shared with her Mum, folded the umbrella, and took off her rain slicker, which she hung in a hallway closet.

Two Hours Later

"She'll never learn," said Robin's mother, Marilyn Sobbs, as she bent over the sink, peering at the dishes Robin had just washed and racked. They could easily afford a dishwasher, but Marilyn believed they wasted water. And she still felt she had to train her daughter, even though Robin was in her mid-forties and would probably always leave a few microscopic smears of food on the plates, crust on the cutlery. It annoyed Robin

174

especially that her mother talked about her in her presence as though she wasn't there.

"She'll never learn because she doesn't want to. And that's something nobody can fix. Not even her dear mum." Robin winced when she said things like that. The shoe, she believed, was on the other foot. The Numinoids only tolerated the likes of Robin's family because their continued skepticism shored up her faith. They encouraged tension, thought it a powerful way to sustain believers. And draw fresh ones.

At least, that was the rumor, because the Numinoids themselves had still to make their agenda known.

"You've never lacked for love and kindness," added Marilyn as she held up a blue-veined China plate to the buzzing fluorescent bulbs set over the sink. She frowned when she saw a hairline fracture. "You really shouldn't use the good dishes for a family dinner, dear. It's just us."

It was all willful insanity; the web of trivial, petty details humanity had enslaved itself to. They had come to free the soul from the flesh, to dig it out and snap it clean at the root. So Robin thought as she smiled and looked up from a quilt she was crocheting. "I'm sorry, were you addressing me, Mum?"

"Don't be smart with me, young lady."

Robin dropped her head. "I'm sorry, Mum. I'll be more careful next time."

"And don't tell me you're unaware of the spidery machines."

"Pardon?"

Marilyn pointed at the window. Robin peered out. "No, I'm afraid they're new to me."

Her Mum sighed; "As I suspected."

IV. New Church of the Body Apocalyptic

"Brothers and sisters in Nuomen, we are gathered today to celebrate the sacrifice of our Lord and Servitor on his special day." The High Priestess lifted the egg from her headpiece and kneeled before the altar, on which the Prime Minister lay flayed, skin flaps nailed into the wood.

He was still awake.

"Through our offering, we will lift the Starbaby from the pyramid's eye," she intoned, and a murmur of accord rumbled through the cathedral.

Above the altar, behind the High Priestess, a wall screen showed the PM's darkest dreams, sourced from his Dream Receptor Sites. Troubadours and clowns unrolled a wet stretch of Moebius Striptease from a girl's body, until her organs glistened and pulsed in painful detail. The worshippers gasped and lowered their heads. A strobing effect, white light flushing out imagery drawn out from the acolytes themselves through smartdust portals, superimposed on the PM's dissected form.

The sacrifice was indeterminate, an endless loop. Revelations glimpsed briefly wriggled back down wormholes burned through the cathedral walls. The cathedral began to rise, lurching forward, and the worshippers spilled across the stained oak floor. Some impaled themselves spontaneously with erotic crucifixes, as the cathedral righted and scudded to a halt just short of the Thames Estuary.

"Only those with true grit will attain to understanding," moaned the Priestess, lifting her shiny black robes to show shaved pussy inset with a razormachine that tickled her labia; tiny droplets of blood oozed down her bare legs.

"That which is mine is yours and mine and Numinosity," chorused the devotees.

"His disease is our salvation." At this, the Priestess dug inside the PM and began to lift out bits, gobbets of organ meat, dog scraps, then deeper, further until she'd wrenched out a few recalcitrant bones. The Prime Minister flat lined, and then jolted back to life again.

"For the love of Christ, stop this insanity!" he screamed.

The Priestess began to throw the morsels into the crowd, who attacked them like jackals, screaming and frothing at the mouth, tearing off their clothes and gouging wounds into their naked bodies as they fell to their haunches and feasted. The worshippers shortly began to transform, as the sins force-fed the PM contorted and danced within them. The call for "more grotesques" had been answered at last. On their hands and knees, they formed a centipedal unit and began to wind their way towards the doors. Fur burst from chests; canines sharpened; demon lights sparkled in their eyes.

Then a shot rang out, felt more than heard, and a massive ripple turned the walls into a waterfall of steel, concrete, and glass.

The Glock had been freed, the jury delivered of their verdict, the state of quantum suspension collapsed, and linearity reigned once again. London Bridge snapped back into place, and the flow of travel continued as though nothing unusual had occurred. Crimes hitherto considered impossible regained a local habitation and a name; evidence separated itself from the methods used to collect and define it, and forensic detectives patted intact and separate identities like beloved lost pets.

The worshippers writhed in agony before the cathedral as they shed their new animalized forms, down to blazing epidermal sacks, which rotted off and squeezed out the bones. But they were not allowed to die, even then, because those effects set in motion before the collapse would have to run their course.

Robin Sobbs never complained again of her dishwashing duties. Chastened, embarrassed and more than a little freaked out by their narrow escape with madness, Her Cybermajesty's government determined to maintain order, symmetry and binary logic at all costs, whatever it took.

And the Numinoids chased their shadows back through the holes they'd punched in space-time, to meditate and philosophize on the fruit of their experiment with human destiny. Mankind, it appeared, was unripe, and millennia would pass until they were ready to be plucked.

Ron Richmond

How a Mental Hospital Reminds Me

of Salvador Dali

Dali was Satan...
At least he had the mustache for the part
And really really weird.
The similarity ends there.
I came into this world of fading
Brick slaughterhouses,
Repositories for the hopelessly confused.
Crumbling walls, rusting and bleeding dust
Into already heavy skies.
I've seen escape tubes dangling from
Vacant windows.
Not knowing their purpose,
Sporting game or cruel hoax,
I expected to see a mad man hurling
Headlong from the opening at any moment.
Distorted faces peering at me
From smudged uneven windows
melting clocks, fallen faces
Begging for a moment's respite
Twisted hands
spasm grasping only emptiness.
I fear his world hopes to melt my soul
Caring not that I am ill-suited to face the judgment of Dali
And madmen hoping to claim some precious prize.
Vive la foile
Or something to that end

Ron Richmond

Proverbs from a Very Confused Mind

Dreams are like raindrops...
Fears
Like sunspots,
Robots, chickens
And kumquats.

People are giving away
Answers for free,
Questioning everything,
Telling me
Nothing.

The clown of nouns and frowns
Expounds
On things he knows
Nothing about.

Why do all of my dreams end
Just before I wake?
They leave me alone
Sleepwalking
In an empty house.

My mouth is full
Of the words I spoke.
This poem is the sum of the letters
I wrote.
336 not including these.

About the Authors

Jaap Boekestein (1968) is an award winning Dutch writer of science fiction, fantasy, horror, thrillers and whatever takes his fancy. Five novels and almost three hundred of his stories have been published. His has made his living as a bouncer, working for a detective agency and as editor. He currently works for the Dutch Ministry of Security and Justice. http://jaapboekestein.com/

William Cook was born and raised in New Zealand and is the author of the novel 'Blood Related,' and two non-fiction books: 'Gaze into the Abyss: The Poetry of Jim Morrison' and 'Secrets of Best-Selling Self-Published Authors.' He has written many short stories that have appeared in anthologies and has authored two short-story collections ('Dreams of Thanatos' & 'Death Quartet') and two collections of poetry ('Journey: the search for something' & 'Corpus Delicti'). William writes horror and thriller fiction mostly, but also ventures into literary fiction, a bit of Sci-fi, Young Adult and, more recently, Non-Fiction.

His work has been praised by Graham Masterton, Joe McKinney, Billie Sue Mosiman, Anna Taborska, Rocky Wood and many other notable writers and editors. William is also the editor of the anthology 'Fresh Fear: Contemporary Horror,' published by James Ward Kirk Fiction.

Member of the Horror Writers Association, Australian Horror Writers Association, SpecFicNZ & the SFFANZ.

To get an email whenever the author releases a new title and/or gives away free books, sign up for the VIP newsletter at: http://williamcookwriter.com/p/subscribe-now.html (just copy and paste into your browser).

"This man is simply scary. There is both a clinical thoroughness and a heartfelt emotional thoroughness to his writing. He manages to shock as well as empathize, to scare as well as acclimatize, yet beneath it all is a well read intelligence that

demands to be engaged. I loved Blood Related. Ordinarily I hate serial killer stories, but William Cook won me over. He is a unique and innovative talent."
- Joe McKinney, Bram Stoker Award-winning author of Flesh Eaters and Dog Days

"William Cook tells a gruesome story with a sense of authenticity that makes you question with considerable unease if it really is fiction, after all."
- Graham Masterton, author of The Manitou and Descendant

#horror #thriller #psychological horror #psychological Thriller #free #youngadult #darkfiction

A. Henry Keene: Writing from his home in Louisville, Kentucky, A. Henry melds pulp fiction style and content with literary concerns. His works include "Belle of the West," and the upcoming Noir detective novella, "Peekaboo." A. Henry co-edited "Terror Train," an anthology, which explores the train in popular imagination and the horror genre.

Aaron Vlek is a storyteller whose work focuses primarily on the trickster mythos in its role as transformer, bringer of delight and proponent of disquieting humors. Most of her (yes, her) short stories, poetry, and novels, center around the goings on of the jinn, and of a universal imagining of the Native American character, Coyote. Some works are historical in setting while others occupy a contemporary and urban landscape. Newer works explore how ideas of good and evil have changed dramatically, and how certain figures, mundane and arcane, can turn this to their advantage. She also indulges from time to time in the reimagining of classic themes of horror and the occult. Aaron is a graduate of Sarah Lawrence College where she spent most of her time writing. She also took numerous writing workshops at Sarah Lawrence Writing Institute. *Domine Canè,* a short piece of speculative horror with a historic theme, appeared in the April 2015 issue of *Bards and Sages Quarterly, Vol. VII, Issue II. The Black Meal,* a work of speculative horror appeared in the October 2015 issue of *Outposts of Beyond. At the Kids' Table* appears in the 2015 Christmas Edition of *Chicken Soup for the Soup.*

Eric LaRocca's fiction has been published in literary publications such as, *Bizzaro Central*, *Dark Moon Digest*, *Infernal Ink*, *Massacre Magazine*, *Sanitarium*, and *The Horror Zine*. His work has been featured in anthologies such as, *Of Devils and Deviants: An Anthology of Erotic Horror* (Crowded Quarantine Publications). He is also the author of several plays that have been produced by Hartford Stage (Hartford, CT), La Petite Morgue (New York, NY), and Gadfly Theatre Productions (Minneapolis, MN). He currently studies at Western Connecticut State University in Danbury, CT. Follow him on Twitter @ejlarocca.

Sheldon Woodbury is an award winning writer (screenplays, plays, books, and short stories) living in New York City, where he also teaches screenwriting at New York University. His books include "Cool Million" a how to guide on high concept screenwriting. His screenplay "The Book of Magic" won first prize in the Maniafest horror screenwriting competition. His latest short stories are "Bones in a City Graveyard" in Bones 2 (JWK Fiction), "Dirty Minds" in Serial Killers Quattuor (JWK Fiction), "The Halloween House" in One Hellacious Halloween (Horror Novel Reviews), "Family Affair" in Clerics, Charlatans & Cultists (Gothic City Press), "Last Call" in Shots of Terror (Angelic Knight Press), "Payback is a Bitch" in We are Dust and Shadow (JWK Fiction), "Between Heaven and Hell" in Demonic Possession (JWK Fiction), "Holy War" in No Sight for the Saved (JWK Fiction), "A Beautiful Horror" in Hell II: Citizens (JWK Fiction), "The Holy Ghost" in Ghosts Revenge (JWK Fiction),"A White Farewell with a Splash of Red" in Once Bitten (KnightWatch Press), "Magic Macabre" in Toys in the Attic (JWK Fiction), and "A Gift from the Stars" in Lovecraft after Dark (JWK Fiction). His flash fiction stories have appeared many times on the website Hellnotes (JournalStone Publishing) and other stories on Popcorn Fiction (Mulholland Books) and Horror Novel Reviews. His article, "Heroes that Rock" appeared in Writer's Digest Magazine. "The World on Fire," his horror novel, was published September, 2014 by JWK Fiction. His poetry has appeared in Dark Gothic Resurrected magazine, Gothic Tales of Terror (Verto Publishing) and other publications.

Trevor Hallam is the author of God Complex, Not Without Remorse: Edited For Content, The Wandering Man, and the forthcoming Satan, Bless Thy Daughters. He lives near Calgary, Alberta.

Essel Pratt is a writer, a dreamer, and a man of chaotic mind. His writings have been highlighted in over fifty anthologies, with that number increasing every year. His first novel Final Reverie was followed up by a children's book called ABC's of Zombie Friendship. Essel refuses to be classified as a genre writer, instead spreading his focus on whatever comes to mind.

Thomas M. Malafarina (www.ThomasMMalafarina.com) is an author of horror fiction from Berks County, Pennsylvania. To date he has published five horror novels "Ninety-Nine Souls", "Burn Phone", "Eye Contact" , "Fallen Stones" and "Dead Kill – Book 1 – The Ridge of Death", as well as seven collections of horror short stories; "Thirteen Nasty Endings", "Gallery Of Horror", "Malafarina Maleficarum Vol. 1", Malafarina Maleficarum Vol. 2", "Ghost Shadows", "Undead Living" and most recently "Malaformed Realities Vol. 1". He has also published a book of often strange single panel cartoons called "Yes I Smelled It Too; Cartoons For The Slightly Off Center". He is currently putting the final touches on his latest novel "Dead Kill Book 2: The Ridge of Change" for publication early 2016. All of his books have been published through Sunbury Press (www.Sunburypress.com). In addition, many of Thomas's works have appeared in dozens of short story Anthologies and e-magazines. Some have also been produced and presented for internet podcasts as well. Thomas is best known for the twists and surprises in his stories and his descriptive often gory passages have given him the reputation of being one who paints with words. Thomas is also an artist, musician, singer and songwriter.

Mathias Jansson is a Swedish art critic and horror poet. He has been published in magazines as The Horror Zine, Dark Eclipse, Schlock and The Sirens Call. He has also contributed to over 100 different horror anthologies from publishers as Horrified Press, James Ward Kirk Fiction, Source Point Press, Thirteen Press etc. Homepage: http://mathiasjansson72.blogspot.se/ Amazon author page: http://www.amazon.co.uk/Mathias-

Jake Walters has been published in several journals. He currently teaches English in Transylvania.

Robert Holt is the author of Death's Disciples, a gruesome horror novel published by JWK Fiction. He has also published a book of short horror stories for toddler aged children titled The Vegetarian Werewolf and Other Stories. He has been writing all of his life and has published hundreds of short stories.

Justin Burkart I am originally an Arkansan, raised by story-telling grandparents in the Ozarks. They gave me folklore and ears. Now, I am a last year MFA candidate at UNH, where some think I hear voices and call me crazy for what I am sending you. It is my hope that you at least have fun with these. Thanks for reading me.

Tom Howard is a science fiction and fantasy short story writer in Little Rock, Arkansas. He thanks his children for inspiration and the Central Arkansas Speculative Fiction Writers' Group for their perspiration.

Stephen McQuiggan was the original author of the bible; he vowed never to write again after the publishers removed the dinosaurs and the spectacular alien abduction ending from the final edit. His first novel, *A Pig's View Of Heaven*, is available now from Grinning Skull Press.

Donald Armfield has an active imagination with vivid story telling. Fueled by coffee and a few other things. He sits under a roof with his family of a wife and four daughters and lets his mind leak out, filling the computer screen with words that turn into stories and poetic lines. His work has appeared in numerous anthologies and blogs. He has his own poetry collection "Jagermeister Walking". A novella "Hung Hounds" and a kindle single "Walkin' After Midnight" Donald can tackle any genre and come rolling out with something that will scare, haunt, laugh out loud or just be out of this world weirdness. Check out his Facebook author page, Amazon and Goodreads Author pages.

Justin Hunter has seven published novels and has been published in over thirty anthologies.

Kyle Rader: I am a full-time writer and have recently completed my first novel 'Four Bullets', which will be published this fall by Mirror Matters Press. Additionally, sixteen of my short stories have been published in a variety of places, including "Dark Moon Digest", "Fiction Vortex", of which my story "The Countess and the Bard" was the recipient of the Readers' Choice Award, and most recently in the "Bugs" and "And Death Shall Have No Dominion: Tales of the Titanic" anthologies edited by Dean M. Drinkel. I can be followed on Twitter @youroldpalkile or my website http://kylerader.net

Dona Fox lives in the western United States near the gold mining fields where men went mad. She has published stories and poems in Eldritch Tales, Haunts, Thin Ice, Cemetery Dance (Issue #1), Beyond, and New Blood magazines. Read more of her stories in James Ward Kirk and J Ellington Ashton Press publications in the States and Dark Chapter Press and Horrified Press in the United Kingdom. Her first collection of short stories, Dark Tales from the Den, was released in 2015 and Darker Tales will be available in 2016.

Calvin Demmer is a crime, mystery, and speculative fiction author. When not writing, he is intrigued by that which goes bump in the night and the sciences of our universe. His work has appeared in a variety of publications including Sanitarium Magazine, Morpheus Tales, and Mystery Weekly Magazine.

Alex S. Johnson is the author of several books, including most recently The Pit and the Void, The Doom Hippies and Doctor Flesh (both Recommended for Bram Stoker nominations), a regular blogger with horroraddicts.net and a frequent guest on Zombiepalooza Dead Again Radio with Jackie Chin. Following in the wake of the successful Floppy Shoes Apocalypse clown horror anthology, Johnson and co-editor Mary Genevieve Fortier (Toys in the Attic) will shortly release the follow-up, Cherry Nose Armageddon, featuring contributions from Stoker-nominated author John Claude Smith, Christopher Ropes (Nightscript Volume 2) and horror legend Ramsey Campbell. Johnson runs

Nocturnicorn Books from his home in Carmichael, California and is an Active Member of Horror Writers Association.

Dona Fox lives in the western United States near the gold mining fields where men went mad. She has published stories and poems in Eldritch Tales, Haunts, Thin Ice, Cemetery Dance (Issue #1), Beyond, and New Blood magazines. Read more of her stories in James Ward Kirk and J Ellington Ashton Press publications in the States and Dark Chapter Press and Horrified Press in the United Kingdom. Her first collection of short stories, Dark Tales from the Den, was released in 2015 and Darker Tales will be available in 2016.

Ron Richmond was born as an infant; he has since grown to an enormous height of over 50 feet, which makes dating very difficult. When he is not idly enjoying his hobbies of writing poetry and listening to the songs of cat's mating he is actually employed at a place where they actually give him money. He currently lives in Richmond, Indiana, which was probably not named after him. His poetry has appeared in *Nomad's Choir* and *Children, Churches and Daddies*.

About the Cover Artist

John D. Stanton

John's photography, poetry, articles and fiction have appeared in The Indianapolis Star, Not One of Us, MIND, Black Petals, Mt. Zion Speculative Fiction Review, Requiem for the Damned, Shadow and Substance, RAZAR I and II, Yellow Mama, Theatre of Decay, Static Movement, and many other publications. In the visual realm, his specialties include historic photo restoration, infrared photography, and stereography. His unique Subtractive Illusion, a stereoscopic demonstration involving color-tint frequencies that cancel each other out in the brain, is featured on Corel.com. During the years John was an IT consultant and ran a DTP business, his articles were published in Computer User, Compuserve Magazine, ST World and ST Express. He also edited various computer newsletters. John has provided hundreds of images to the small press, electronic and print editions, and book covers, earning Top Ten Finisher in the annual Predator and Editor polls, as well as three mentions in Ellen Datlow's "Best of" collections. John taught an editing class at Marian University with his wife Flo. The two artists stalk abandoned warehouses, factories, graveyards, and other haunted sites where they find bizarre inspiration for their photographic, audio, and literary creations.

About the Illustrator Gidion Van de Swaluw

Gidion van de Swaluw is a Dutch artist and illustrator. He lives in the Netherlands where he studied fine arts at the art-academy in Kampen. Nowadays he focuses especially on drawing and painting bizarre landscapes and the absurd creatures that inhabit them. When asked where he gets his inspiration, he usually tells people 'I paint 'em like I see 'em pop up all around me.' He has produced cover and interior art for a few dozen horror and fantasy books and magazines and he is a regular supplier of bizarro art for the biggest Dutch Sci-Fi magazines.

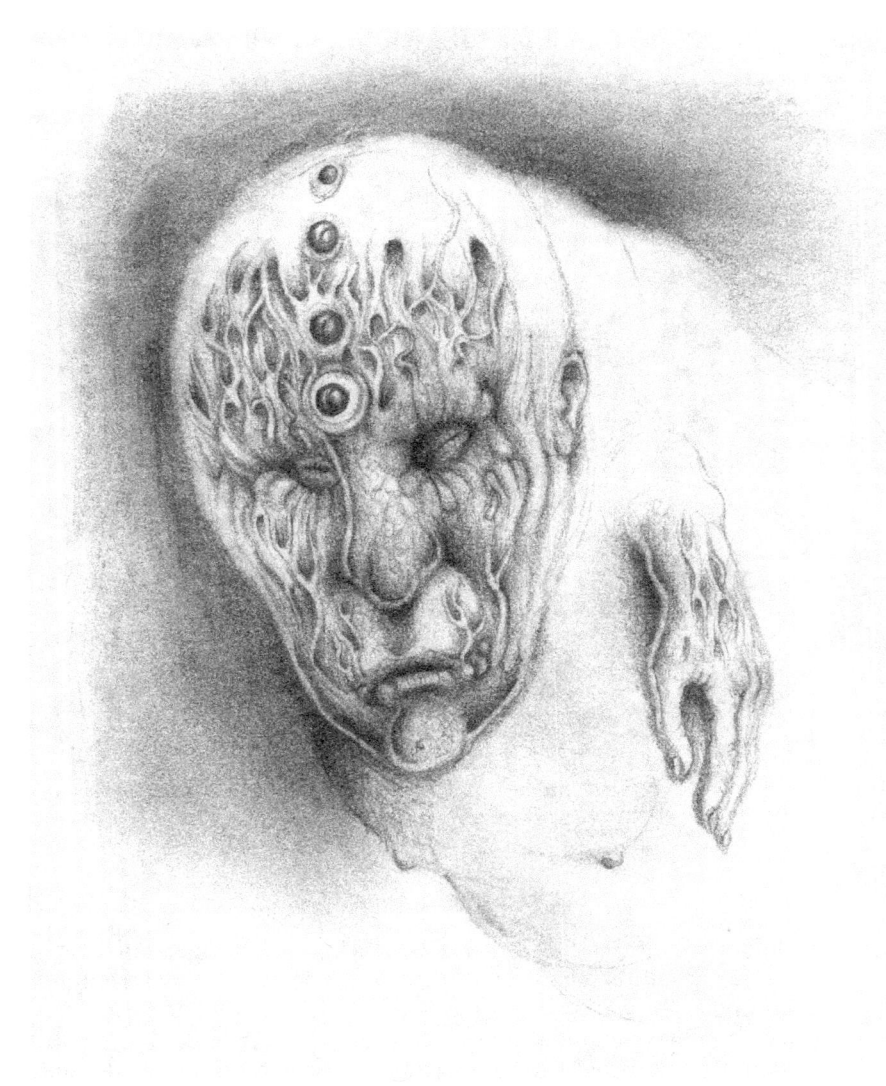

190

www.ingramcontent.com/pod-product-compliance
Lightning Source LLC
Chambersburg PA
CBHW070019260626
47159CB00005B/1883